THE **BAYONET SCARS** FINALE

CEASE

Love is never more real than when it's forever.

JC EMERY

JC Emery

Series & Titles By JC Emery

Bayonet Scars
Ride (No. 1)
Thrash (No. 2)
Rev (No. 3)
Crush (No. 4)
Vow (No. 4.5)
Burn (No. 5)
Crave (No. 5.5)
Haunt (No. 6)
Cease (No. 7)

MATURE CONTENT WARNING
The Bayonet Scars novels are a dark and gritty romance series which features graphic sexual content, violence, and foul language that is intended for a mature audience. Each novel features a different couple, though it's not recommended that they be read out of order due to the series story arc.

JC Emery

CEASE (THE BAYONET SCARS FINALE)
Copyright © 2016 by Christina Emery

All rights reserved. This book may not be reproduced, scanned, or distributed in any printed or electronic form without permission from the author. Please do not participate in or encourage piracy of copyrighted materials in violation of the author's rights. All characters and storylines are the property of the author and your support and respect if appreciated. The characters and events portrayed in this book are fictitious. Any similarity to real persons, living or dead, is coincidental and not intended by the author.
ISBN: 1541059484
ISBN-13: 978-1541059481

Cover Design by Brenda Gonet at Star Bound Books
Formatting by Christina Emery www.jcemery.com
Editing by Michele Milburn

JC Emery

DEDICATION

For Dawn.

For the last three years of f-bombs, unruly characters, and screwdrivers in inappropriate places.

CONTENTS

	Acknowledgments	i
2016	Chapter 1	1
1997	Chapters 2-8	4
2016	Chapter 9	101
1997	Chapter 10	108
1994	Chapter 11	120
1997	Chapters 12-15	141
1998	Chapters 16-17	203
1999	Chapter 18	230
2005	Chapter 19	238
2014	Chapter 20	249
2016	Chapters 21-22	254
	Epilogue I & II	286

ACKNOWLEDGMENTS

Seven novels, a novella, a novelette, and a half a million words later, and here we are, saying goodbye to the Bayonet Scars series. After spending the last four years in these characters' heads, I'm not sure I know how to say goodbye. But I do know that you— the reader— have given me more than you'll ever know. So many of you have become my friends and I'd be lost without you.

Dawn, I blame these nine volumes on you and your constant encouragement to add "just one more" book. No, we're not going for an even ten. You're cut off. Mom, this has been a crazy ride, hasn't it? From that time little baby me slid out of your vagina to the day I mentioned outlaw bikers and I swear you listened to me talk for the first time in your life, we've been through a lot.

Mandie, you're awesome and you know why. I'm not getting sappy with your salty ass. Brenda at Star Bound Books, your covers are the reason people took notice of these books. You've been with me on this journey longer than anyone. Michele, you're a fantastic editor and a gracious friend. I love your notes in the margins and attempts at getting me to understand proper hyphen usage.

Dani, you get the first actual thank you here, and it's for not smothering me in my sleep or paying someone else to do it. I'm disorganized and perpetually late with everything, but you still seem to like me. Thank you for taking a chance on me as your first client and as your friend, I'm insanely proud to be part of your journey. Nazarea, I only have one thing to say to you. Destiel will be canon in Season 13 or we riot.

And to everybody else who didn't get called out by name, I love you. Thank you for being a part of this strange life I get to live. Thank you all for everything. I can't believe we're saying goodbye to the Forsaken Motorcycle Club, but I'm so grateful that we've taken this ride.

Now, if you'll excuse me, Leo's calling…

CHAPTER ONE

Ruby
Brooklyn, New York
April 2016
Mancuso's downfall

Time after time, I never cease to be amazed at how deeply I can be hurt.

Just a flesh wound, Mama.

Jim's words echo in my mind over and over again. They're all I hear as I watch my husband—the man who taught me that men can be good—being lifted into the back of the van by his brothers. Blood pools at the bottom of his vest and drips to the pavement.

My daughter—the precious baby I thought I'd lost forever—is being carried to the van by the boy who became my son at the age of eight. She's lost so much blood. The dark red liquid completely covers her face, neck, and chest. My heart falls into my stomach as I catch sight of the blood smeared all over Ryan's cut and his face.

My husband's been gutted, and my daughter's been sliced open.

Both bleeding.

One dying.

Maybe two.

Hopefully none.

And all I can think about is my own selfish need to keep them with me. If I'm not a mother to my daughter or a wife to my husband, then I don't know who I am. I'll still have my sons—all three of them—but it's not the same. My boys don't need me the way my man and my girl do. I won't get to hang on to Michael for much longer. He's a Mancuso, and he'll be staying in New York to take over the family—and it doesn't matter how I feel about that. Ian, my eldest, has his wife, Mindy. He thinks he still needs me, but he doesn't. Ryan, the boy I have to remind myself isn't really mine, has Alex. *My daughter.*

If we lose her, there's nothing anyone can do to make it better. Ryan will never recover, and neither will I. He'll shut down, just like Rage did when we lost Sylvia, and even I won't be able to reach him then.

If we lose Jim, we lose our rock. I lose the only person I ever trusted enough to give my whole heart to besides my children.

I won't survive it.

CHAPTER TWO

Phoenix, Arizona
March 1997

The ache in my jaw doesn't dull even after I swallow what he gives me and lick my lips. A fake smile plasters itself on my face, my eyes shine, and I give him a little purr. His dick is tiny as fuck, but all the coke he did is making my job much harder than it has to be. If I didn't need this so much—if it wasn't for my boy—I wouldn't be here. My stomach rolls at the satisfied smile that rests on the strange man's lips, but I power through my disgust and move to crawl up his body. I'm stopped short of his mangled, dirty face by the sharp pain that radiates from my scalp. He threads his fingers through my hair, gripping it closer to my flesh, and gives a hard yank. My eyes narrow before I can stop them. I compliment the way he tastes to smooth things over, but it's too late. He's already seen the look, and he's not having it.

"You're supposed to be a compliant little whore, so act like it." A drop of saliva hits my cheek as he spits the words down at me. I don't flinch or look away. He wants me to back down, but I don't. I can't show any anger or fear. I've spent the last couple of months trying to be his club's perfect little whore so I could earn my ride to California. And it hasn't been easy. Of all the clubs I've hooked up with, his is probably the most depraved and disgusting I've stepped foot in. I need out, and not just for me. My boy is depending on me to get him a little slice of stable, so it doesn't matter how much I hate this man, I'm going to swallow every drop he gives me, and I'll do it with a fucking smile if it means I can get Ian a little bit better.

"You want that ride to California?"

I nod my head and lick my lips eagerly, like I'm some kind of stupid dog that doesn't know danger when she sees it. His eyes fall to my lips, and he loosens his grip on my hair just slightly. Just enough to give me some relief.

"Talk, bitch," he says. There's food between his teeth. His breath is foul. I hate this guy, but since I got here, he's been the most aggressive about getting me into bed. I've let him have his fill plenty of times, but once I realized this place was no good for my boy, I started making it more difficult for him to get me back to his room. So far, my plan has worked. He's more desperate than ever to get a hold of me, but if he wants what I have, he's going to have to deal to get it.

"I want the ride to California, and you want my pussy. We made a deal..." I come close to saying his name, but I'm not even sure I know it, so I stop short. To emphasize my point, I rub my hands on the tops of his thighs. He watches my hands while he makes me wait for an answer.

"You want that ride, you're gonna have to fucking earn it."

And I do. I take everything he gives me, only wincing once when I can't block out how rough he's being. I do what I do every time a man takes me to bed—I just mentally detach from my body and go through the motions. I purr when I'm supposed to, I tell them I love the way they feel, and I so scream loudly when I'm supposed to be orgasming that they puff their chests out with pride. I take them however they want, again and again, and I don't complain. I leave my son with other whores, and I drop to my knees if that's what they want. Anytime. Anywhere. And I scrub their scents off of me every single night, but it never goes away.

And it doesn't matter, because a kid can't eat off of love. My devotion to my boy won't buy him new shoes when his are worn out. I don't have any marketable skills, an education, or any luck in picking friends, so I just do what I need to, take what I must, and find a way to live with the consequences of how I choose to survive.

Even when it leaves me bruised and raw and wincing every time I move, like now.

The disgusting pig behind me grunts as he slams into me, his fingers digging into my hips. The sound of skin slapping against skin sends a shiver up my spine, but not for the reason the man thinks. He's close to coming, and I silently thank his sad little dick because his lack of girth is about the only thing saving me from running out of here right now. Just as his body begins to shake, there's a loud banging on the bedroom door. There isn't a working lock, so whoever is banging is at least being semi-courteous. The man ignores it, grunts loudly, and holds on to me tighter. I lower my head, breathing in and out slowly, trying to keep myself from screaming. He wants me to lose it, to break down and beg for him to stop. The sick fuck gets off on that shit, but I won't do it. I refuse to give that to him.

The door flies open, bringing in a gush of cool air the stings my naked body. I try not to look up to meet the intruder's eyes, but it's too difficult. A woman stands in the doorway, the same woman I left Ian with. When I told her my name is Ruby, she told me her name is Gem. Which sounds like total bullshit, but I went with it. She's coked-up half the time, got a cock in her the other half, but she likes kids and she's been good to mine, so I've relied on her since I got here. Only tonight, I shouldn't have left Ian. He was in one of his moods. I told myself this is a means to an end and left even though she didn't look like she was in a good place. It was better than leaving him alone when he's like that, though, so I did it. And now, just by looking at her, I know I fucked up and made the wrong choice. Gem's eyes are frantic, and she's shaking slightly. She's got fresh, bloody scratches up and down her arms.

"It's Ian," is all she says, but it's enough. I scramble to get away from Tiny Dick, but he frantically grabs for my hair and pulls it hard, keeping me in place. Instead of helping or saying anything,

Gem stands in the doorway, watching Tiny Dick slam into me, his portly body shaking in the process, as he rides out his orgasm. I should feel humiliated, disgusted with myself. Instead, all I can feel is fear. Gem wasn't all scratched up when I left Ian at the motel with her. She seemed fine, chill even, despite Ian's mood. Now she looks like she's been through hell and back. Even her once perfectly-applied makeup has taken a beating this evening. Thick black smudges surround her eyes, and her bright pink lipstick is worn off, though only halfway.

When Tiny Dick finally finishes, he pulls out and shoves me forward onto the floor. I land awkwardly, my shoulder hitting the wood floor first. I force myself to ignore the pain as I scramble into my jeans and top, totally ignoring my underwear and only grabbing my bra as an afterthought. As I dress, Gem tells me that she left Ian in the motel room by himself. That she didn't know what to do. That she was close to calling an ambulance.

"We leave at eight," Tiny Dick says as I rush out of the room and toward the motel as quickly as I can. I don't even stop for my shoes—a cheap pair of dollar sandals I bought at Goodwill in the last city we stayed in—and run out of the clubhouse barefoot. It's close to midnight, but thanks to record highs, the ground is still warm to the touch. I stumble just slightly as I step into the busy road but don't let myself fall. Correcting myself quickly, I dodge an oncoming motorcycle and run at full speed across the hot blacktop, over rocks and other sharp objects I can't see, through the motel parking lot, and up the stairs to our second-floor room.

I stop only when I'm at the open door. I should run in. I should ignore the desperate cries and the crashing sounds. But I can't. Ian's moods range from sweet and quiet to destructive and insane. He's been through hell, and he's not quite back yet. I can't blame him, but I know better than to barge in on him when he's losing his shit. The last time I got him to a doctor, they said he was tall for his age. That was a while ago, and it's been at least six months since I needed to get him back in. It's not easy finding a free clinic to check him out when we have no permanent address and my driver's license is from New York and has been expired for a year.

Slowly, I walk into the room and call out to my boy as I survey the damage. The two bedside lamps have been knocked over, one completely broken and the other just tipped. The Bible that sat in the bedside table is scattered around the room, the back and front half of the book on the floor near the TV,

Cease (the Bayonet Scars finale)

with the rest of the pages covering the floor and the bed. I notice the word *sin* scrawled in Ian's messy handwriting etched into the pages. And on the white walls. And even on the dresser, though it's hard to tell there since all he had handy was a black ballpoint. This is everything I fear but nothing surprising. Six months we've been doing this—cycling through one meltdown after another—and no matter what I do, it's never enough. One psychologist said my boy needs to be hospitalized, but we tried that and he only regressed. They wanted him to talk about his trauma, to explain in detail what happened to him. Fuck them and their bullshit. My boy won't talk about it, and I won't make him. It's bad enough he had to live through what that sick fuck did to him. They always want to know where his scars come from. I always want to ask which ones they're talking about—the ones they can see or the ones they can hear.

It's bad enough that I can't down enough Jack or take enough dick or do enough lines to block out the memories of that bastard touching my son. I won't make Ian talk it out with a goddamn stranger, even if it means we handle this on our own and in our own dysfunctional way.

I stop just before I reach the closed bathroom

door and try to get Ian's attention again. He's still screaming, frantically, at the top of his lungs. His voice is hoarse, but he doesn't stop. He never does, not until he's good and ready. Knowing this could be a while, I take my place on the other side of the door and clear my throat. This is our routine—the only way he'll recognize me when he's like this. I start to sing. It's a stupid little song about bunnies in the forest, and I think its message is about not being a bully or some shit. I don't know, but when Ian was in kindergarten, he taught it to me, and he likes it when I sing it to him. In the last year he started telling me he likes the song because it's about getting back at someone. I don't think it is, but I let him believe what he wants, even if it is totally fucked for an eight-year-old to believe in vengeance. I should be teaching him better, I should be giving him more. I should be doing a lot of things, but instead, I just sit on that dingy motel carpet and scream-sing at the top of my lungs. Eventually Ian's voice falters and lowers, though he doesn't stop. I'm coughing through what I think might be the hundredth rendition of the song when Ian quiets and then stops. I lower my voice but keep singing. Tears sting at my eyes, but I hold them back when he opens the door and crawls out of the bathroom. His brown eyes are filled with tears, and he's got bright red, raised streaks across his cheeks and arms. My heart sinks at the sight, but I only bumble the words a little before I get back on track and force myself to keep singing. If I get too upset, he'll turn around and go back into the bathroom, and then it'll take another hour to get him out. This isn't about me—this is about a little boy who's scared and traumatized and doesn't know how to express any of it, so he just flips out and destroys everything, including himself.

When he's finally in my arms, I hold him tight against me, barely giving him room to breathe. Even when he pushes against me, I don't let him go. I just tell him what he needs to hear, never stopping until he takes a deep breath and drifts off to sleep.

"Clean, clean, clean," I chant as he dozes off as if saying the word will erase the sin he feels in his heart. Once his breathing has stabilized, I haul him into the bed and go about cleaning up the room. I get as much antiseptic on his scratches as I can, but he stirs too much, so I save that for the morning. When everything is as tidy as it's going to get, I crawl into the bed and wrap my body around my poor, broken little boy and cry as silently as I can so not to wake him.

"Tomorrow we leave for California. Things will be better there," I whisper through the sobs that rack my body. "It'll be better. It will. I promise."

CHAPTER THREE

Jim
Fort Bragg, California
March 1997

My eyes scan the main room of the clubhouse, surveying the sea of leather crowded inside. There's a tightness in my chest with this many guys in here, and it doesn't help that more than half of them aren't even Forsaken. Fucking Arizona shows up with the whole goddamn charter in tow. These bastards need to learn that their dick size doesn't mean shit this far north. I have to tolerate them, though. Rage gets his prick hairs all knotted up if we start shit with other clubs for "no reason." Like having a bunch of orange, leathery-looking bitches up in my space isn't reason enough for shit to hit the fan.

"Don't like seeing this many strange fucks in my clubhouse." Sterling Grady, our newest patched member, walks up to me. His eyes slide from one side of the room to another, and the corner of his top lip is curled up in disgust. The kid is barely twenty years old with more brawn than brains and an attitude to match.

"*Your* clubhouse, Sterling?"

He doesn't take the bait—something he's never done before—and it leaves me on edge until I follow his gaze across the room. Chief, Grady's surrogate dad, who's really better aged to be an older brother figure, is staring him down and shaking his head. Only person who can give this prick any kind of perspective is Chief, and thank fuck for it, too. Otherwise I'd have choked him by now.

By Chief's side is his wife, Lona, who has an arm wrapped protectively around their daughter, Elle. Chief gives Lona a quick nod, mutters a few words, and sees them to the door. Right on their heels is my fucking kid. Ryan's just turned nine, and he's already hard up for Elle, who's just two years older than he is. I ignore the kid as he follows them out the door and decide to actually take care of shit so these assholes can get out of my clubhouse.

I'm in the middle of finalizing a deal with one of our visitors when Ryan runs back into the room shouting, "Dad! Dad! Dad!" at the top of his lungs. My entire body stiffens at the noise. As it is, Rage doesn't like having him around all the time. Don't know what he thinks I'm going to do with his grandson if I don't have him at the clubhouse, but whatever. It's called parenting, and it's not like I have Ryan's whore of a mother hanging around to make sure the kid eats and doesn't chop off a limb or something. Sensing Rage's agitation even from across the room, I stop what I'm doing and head toward my son. The moment he realizes I'm heading his way, he rushes back out the door. Fuck. The kid gets himself in more trouble than any other kid I know. At least when his friend Josh is around, my boy is less likely to do something to get his ass sent to juvie.

Once I'm outside, I find Ryan standing on the bench of one of the wooden picnic tables that sit between the clubhouse and the fence separating our private parking lot from the Forsaken Custom Cycle lot out in front. A woman stands in front of him, bouncing nervously from foot to foot, and she's got a kid hiding behind her. Ryan doesn't seem to notice or care about the kid. He's all smiles and attitude with the woman. I can see what he sees in her. She's short, but probably not so much for a woman, and she's got long reddish-brown hair that hangs over her shoulders in waves. Even from here, I can see the way her old, worn jeans cling to every curve. She's young but not young enough to cause me problems, so that's a good thing. Despite her small figure and slight curves, she's got a healthy set of tits that look like they're threatening to escape her faded and torn black tank top. The top hangs loose everywhere but her chest, and fuck me if it ain't a sight for sore eyes.

The mystery woman turns her head toward me and blinks rapidly, shock registering on her face before she composes herself and musters up a fake as fuck smile. I know that smile. Ryan's mom was a pro, so I recognize when I'm being played. I try not to let it get to me, but I fail miserably. When her big brown eyes land on mine, she doesn't let go. Latching on to me with her gaze, she stands a little straighter, forcing her tits to strain against the top even more than they were before.

My feet manage to carry me two steps closer to her before they falter, and I stand there in place. I'm so tired of the lost girls we have here. We've been needing fresh meat for a while now, and the way my dick is reacting to this new bitch is proof the situation is worse than I thought. In an attempt to force my dick to chill out, I drag my nails over the scruff on my face, trying to distract myself from how much I like the way this strange woman looks, but it doesn't work. Her eyes catch the move, and her mouth falls open slightly. I watch as her tongue peeks out before she tries to cover her reaction by dragging her teeth over her bottom lip and clearing her throat.

"Sorry for being back here. The kid, uh, Ryan, kind of dragged us," she says. Her voice is soft but purposefully so, with smoky, sultry undertones that I can fucking guarantee come out during sex.

"Dad, she's from Arizona!" Ryan shouts. I ignore him.

"Not a problem. You got a name, beautiful?"

"Ruby."

Fuck me. I even like her name. Within seconds, I'm at her side and staring my kid down like he's the competition. He still hasn't stopped talking even though she's barely listening.

"We always need hotties to clean up around here," Ryan says. My eyes widen and I redirect my attention to him. He doesn't look my way. Instead, he keeps focusing on Ruby. Is my kid...

He can't be doing what I think he's doing.

"Take the job, honey. I'm sure we can work out some form of... compensation... later." My nine-fucking-year-old son winks at Ruby like he's grown or some shit. Before I can stop myself, I reach out and grab my kid behind his neck and yank him off the bench. He hunches over and turns his face to me, giving me a downright dirty-looking glare. Little asshole.

"Shut up while you have the option," I bark loudly in his face. Fucking kid just stares back at me. Doesn't even blink or shriek back from how loud I'm being. Slowly, a shit-eating grin creeps to his lips. There's a twinkle in his eye that hasn't been there since the last time I busted him trying to light an M80.

"It's okay," she says quickly. Her body curves inward and her torso bends slightly toward my boy. Her eyes dart from me to him and back to me again. "I don't want any trouble. I'm just looking for a job, but if you're full up, it's fine."

"You got any skills?"

"I can clean, tend bar. I'll do whatever."

Somehow, by the grace of God or some shit, I manage to not ask her anything crude. I deserve a goddamn medal or something for it, too. The way she looks at me, all serious with a side of desperation, is like catnip for my dick or something.

"Clubhouse is filthy. Pay is shit. You'd be around a bunch of assholes all day."

I don't know a single thing about this woman, aside from her name, and I'm offering her a job. Rage would be taking a swing at me right now if he were out here. I could always sacrifice the kid to him when he finds out, since it was Ryan's idea after all.

"This is not the first club I've been with, but I'm hoping it's the last. I'm just looking to provide for my boy, get him a little normal."

I don't bother telling her that Forsaken is anything but normal for a kid. My attention falls to my own son before I catch sight of her son. He's got large brown eyes beneath a mop of light brown hair, pale skin, and a bridge of freckles across his nose. He looks too skinny to be healthy, and he seems skittish from the way he's desperately clinging to the waistband of his mom's jeans. I give him a half smile, hoping he'll let go of the damn woman for a second, but he doesn't budge.

"You can stay in our house, Ruby," Ryan offers.

"Son, shut your pie hole." I rack my brain but can't figure out what's gotten into him. Ryan's normally quiet until he's got something smart to say. But right now he's being talkative as hell, and it's making me suspicious.

"Thank you, honey, but we have a place to stay." Ruby keeps her voice light, but it feels forced, like she's hiding something.

"Where?"

"Excuse me?"

She blinks at my question as though she didn't hear it. I've spent enough time watching men lie to my face to know she's stalling.

"Where are you staying?"

"Oh, there's a motel down the road."

I know there's a motel down the road, but it's a shit hole. I tell her as much, but she doesn't give. Instead, she just says, "We've stayed in worse."

"You came in from Arizona? What're you doing with those assholes?"

"Just passing through. Ian wanted to come out to California." She reaches around and place a hand on her son's shoulder, giving him a comforting pat.

"Where'd you come from before Arizona?"

"Texas. Is this the background check?" Ruby purses her lips and gives me a sly smile.

I shake my head and rub the back of my neck awkwardly. Her story is full of holes and half-truths, but I don't push. The boy has a backpack strapped to his shoulders, and Ruby's got a medium-sized suitcase by her feet. I'm willing to bet these two bags are all they have in the world, which turns my stomach in some fucked-up way. Fuck. Being a parent is hard enough with all the support I have from my mom and the club. I can't imagine doing it all alone with basically nothing in this world. Nobody should have to live like that, especially not some poor fucking kid. I try to shrug it off by reminding myself that she's going to be working in the clubhouse, so I'll have time to get the rest of the story out of her. I'll just have to stay close enough to make sure she and the kid have enough to survive on.

Finally regaining my ability to speak, I smirk at her. "No. You'll know it when I'm checking you out." She flushes and clears her throat but quickly regains her stoic appearance. I should let her stay in the clubhouse tonight, but the fucking Arizona club is in town and will be partying through the night, so I go ahead and do the dumbest thing I can. "Work tomorrow. You'll ride in with me. Tonight, you'll stay with us."

"I don't need—" she starts.

I cut her off immediately.

"We're not good enough to shelter you for a night, guess we're not good enough to hire you."

Ruby looks down at Ian, whose face peeks out a little more, displaying a large, angry-looking scar that covers almost half his face. I suck in a deep breath, trying to imagine what could have happened to the poor kid. Ruby gives her boy a smile and then another pat.

"Thank you," she says, her attention now back on me. Her eyes are gentle, her voice is firm, and everything about her demeanor tells me she's suddenly relieved. Her shoulders slump, but her chin stays high. The tension around her eyes dissipates.

She had nowhere to go.

Fuck.

Cease (the Bayonet Scars finale)

Who is this woman, and what the hell am I going to do with her?

CHAPTER FOUR

Ruby

"That's my dad," Ryan says. He's still bouncing on the balls of his feet, his big gray eyes trained on me.

"I see the resemblance." Giving the kid a soft smile, I think through my options. Once those assholes from Arizona practically kicked us out of the van, I didn't know where we were going or how we were going to get there. We'd passed a cheap motel on our way through town, but there was no sign telling me how cheap cheap really is in

California. Between the money I've been hoarding and the cash I've managed to collect from the Arizona club before we left, I have about five hundred bucks. Without a job, that's not even going to get us through the month. Sure, Ryan's dad kind of offered me a job. Well, it's more like Ryan offered the job and his dad kind of just... didn't argue it.

Ryan's dad.

That man is trouble, I can already tell. He's tall and muscular but not bulking in a gross, steroids kind of way. I hate when there's so many muscles that the poor guy no longer even has a neck. Ryan's dad—crap, I really need to find out the man's name—is just attractive. Like his son, he has gray eyes with jet-black hair and a pale complexion. He's everything I would have been attracted to before I stopped allowing myself to want anything.

"Ryan!" A loud, smoky, feminine voice shouts from the other side of the parking lot. I focus in on who it's coming from. A middle-aged woman is standing beside a shiny, new-looking truck. She's clutching a large leather purse to her shoulder. Her eyes are narrowed, her head tilting in a way that suggests she's sizing me up.

"That's my grandma," Ryan says with a half smile

on his face. He doesn't move until she calls him again and adds, "Now," in a firm voice. Looking flustered, he jumps off the bench and drags himself away. I turn away as the chatty little boy and his grandma argue about something. They're too far away for me to hear the exact disagreement, but I can come up with something compelling enough. She probably doesn't want her grandson talking to some strange woman, and I don't blame her.

Before I embarrass myself by begging for that job and a place to stay, I take Ian by the hand and head out of the parking lot. If I want things to change, then I need to change the way I go about doing things.

We're halfway to the motel before he gives my hand a tug and stops moving his little feet.

"What's up, baby?"

"I don't like it here," he says, his small voice breaking at the end. I suck in a deep breath to calm myself down. Ian never likes anywhere at first. Well, actually, he just doesn't like anywhere no matter how long we're there for. But eventually something is going to have to give. At some point he's going to have to make peace with the fact that we can change the zip code, the weather, and the club we're with, but we can't just change our damage. He's too young to understand that concept, and I don't expect him to. Still, it's frustrating as hell to go through this every place we go. It's selfish and shitty, but I just want him to—just one fucking time—make me feel like I'm doing an okay job instead of destroying his entire world every single day.

"I know, baby," I say evenly. I bend down so we're eye to eye and cup his cheek with my hand. "I know I keep promising things will get better and they haven't yet. And I'm sorry you don't like it here. We'll keep looking for a place you'll like, okay? Okay, baby?"

"Okay."

And just like that, with that one little word, we're walking again. Some people hate the word *fine* because when most people say they're fine, what they really mean is that things are shit but they're not up for emotionally bleeding all over the place. Ian doesn't say *fine*. He says *okay*. And I guess, after traveling in a hot van all day, that *okay* is better than having a meltdown. I still don't like it, though.

One day, I'm going to make my little boy smile. One day we're going to have our own apartment that I can pay for all by myself. One day we'll buy the brand name foods in the grocery store, and we won't worry about things like not having a phone. One day we're going to live like regular people, and I'll be that mom who cries when her baby walks across the stage at his high school graduation. And one day my boy will tell me he's fine instead of okay, and when he smiles, it won't be to mask how much pain he's in.

One day, I resolve to myself.

Our new life starts today. It starts with me standing on my own two feet and walking us to this motel. It starts with a proper job hunt tomorrow. I'm not sure what I'll do about Ian. He's half a year behind in school because of all the moving and everything else going on. It's a damn miracle that's all he's missed. He needs to catch up, but the year's almost over, and then it'll be summer. I can't leave Ian with just anyone, or he'll flip out, and I can't afford to pay anyone with a license. Plus there's that whole thing about him not being enrolled in school right now. I have enough problems without the law getting all up in my shit. Damn it. This is how I keep ending back up with whatever club is local. Bikers don't give a shit if I have my kid with me at the clubhouse as long as my boy's not in the room while I'm letting them fuck me. Not that I would do that, but the Arizona club's president literally told me that the first time I met him. Sometimes, like right now, it feels too fucking hard to go straight. I have to, though. I want Ian to complain about homework and girls and dumb-ass shit like that. He deserves better, and that means I have to do better. If I want him to stop having nightmares, that means I have to stop putting him in situations that give him those nightmares.

"What's wrong, Mommy?" Ian looks up at me with his big brown eyes narrowed and his lips formed into a pout.

"Sometimes it's hard being a parent," I say.

Thoughtfully, he nods and gives my hand a squeeze, declaring, "Sometimes it's hard being a kid, too."

CHAPTER FIVE

"Okay, and jump!" Ian's got a hold of my pinky, and when I shout for him to jump, he gives it a squeeze. He does this sometimes, holding my pinky instead of my hand. My boy hesitates for a moment as he stares down at the massive puddle in front of us. Sure, it's a big puddle, but the kid's got some ridiculously long legs. I raise an eyebrow, free my pinky, and make a great show of leaping over the puddle. On the other side now, I puff out my chest and put my hands on my hips. With a large, dramatic smile on my face, I stare down at my boy.

"I win!"

"We weren't racing." Ian's eyes are narrowed.

One of the best ways I've found to get him to focus on what's going on around us instead of the monsters that haunt him is to give him something to do. Anything, really, and he's usually fine. He likes to keep busy.

"Yes, we were."

We so weren't.

"You're a cheat!"

"Are you calling your mother a cheat?" I snicker and shake my head at him in mock disbelief.

Here's the thing about my boy—he's sweet and loving and sensitive, but he's also mischievous and ornery, and he has a strong sense of justice.

"Just calling it like I see it." There's a dangerous twinkle in his eye that I don't catch until it's too late. He jumps up in the air and lands right in the middle of the puddle. Dirty water splashes everywhere, soaking my shoes and the bottom half of my jeans. Ian's jeans and shirt are completely drenched, but at least they're not DOA like his only pair of shoes are.

My nose scrunches up and my brow furrows, but I swallow back the angry rant that threatens to escape. It's not easy.

"Shit," I say much too harshly. I didn't budget for shoes, even if he is due for a new pair. Frustration wells in my chest and gets comfortable. I try to ignore it, but it's not working. I can't catch a break no matter what corners I cut or how hard I hustle for an extra couple of bucks. Every time I turn around the kid needs something else. This time it's shoes, but before this it was underwear, and before that, it was jeans because he kept climbing the low brick wall at the park and tearing them up. No matter how many times I try to remind him that we have to take care of our things because I can't afford to keep replacing them, he's still hard on his shit. He's an eight-year-old boy, and I know it's going to happen, but that doesn't make the money just materialize out of nowhere to pay for it all.

When I finally calm down enough to look at my boy, he's got his eyes trained on the ground and his arms straight down by his sides. If I were really mad and not just giving up on the idea of ever getting ahead, he'd already be in tears and running away. I try so hard to not be that mom who yells all the time, but I slip sometimes, and when I do, it tears us both up. Those are the days where I wonder if I should even have him. Not that I'd give him up now. The state would throw my boy away and label him because of his behavioral issues. I don't care if I have to steal everything he needs for the rest of my life. I won't let him fall into the clutches of a greedy asshole who just wants to collect a paycheck.

"Hey, shit happens, right?" I say and ruffle Ian's dark blond hair. He goes stock still and doesn't look up despite my casual tone. I need to stop the impending meltdown. I don't have the energy for it today. Skipping the whole pick-me-up speech and ignoring the fact that I'm going to pay for this later, I swoop down and pull my boy into a bear hug. When he doesn't fight me, I lift him off the ground with a deep breath and settle him into my arms. He's not such a little boy anymore, and that's never more apparent than when I carry him. It takes a long moment, but eventually he settles against me, snuggles his face into my neck, and wraps his arms around me.

"I love you, Snot."

I feel the smile against my neck before he whispers, "Love you more, Booger."

"Do not," I declare, giving him a squeeze. He squeezes me back and settles against me once again. I'd thought he would have asked me to stop with calling him Snot by now, but he hasn't. My muscles ache from the exertion of hauling around a growing boy who's more than half my size, but my heart is warm. A lot of kids wouldn't be cool with me snuggling them in public, but not my kid. He doesn't care who's watching or what's going on. My sweet boy with his gentle heart. He's too soft for this world. I know I can't protect him forever and that eventually the world will get its way and harden him, but he's already been through so much, and I'm going to do everything in my power to keep him sweet for as long as I can.

I walk us into the office of the motel we've been staying at and look around. The aged Formica counter is devoid of paperwork for the first time all week, and Robert, the day clerk, is MIA. The owner's paid more attention to the interior of the common areas than the individual rooms, but even those are outdated and worn. Still, it's a roof over our heads and there's hot water, so I'm not going to complain. The day clerk has been flying solo since we got here, and he's let me exchange maid services for a free room, but this morning he called up to the room to ask me to stop by the office. I've been tense since that call, worried that he's going to ask for more than just maid service in the exchange. It wouldn't be the first time a man used his power to manipulate me into doing something I don't want to do.

My arms are practically numb, my knees ache, and my calves are burning by the time muffled shouting erupts from somewhere in the back. Behind the counter is a small cubby-like area with an opening on the left for access to the lobby and a door in the back for the manager's office. Ian tenses in my arms, so I rub his back, and he calms down not long after. The manager's office door swings open.

"You don't want to lose anything else, you'll do as you're told." A deep, angry voice barks out the order. There's something familiar about it that I can't quite place until I see the person the voice belongs to. Barging out of the office is that Ryan kid's dad, the way too smooth and attractive biker I met on my first day in town. I'd successfully avoided him and his club since that meeting, not that it's been easy. The club owns this town, that much is obvious from the little bit we've seen of the town. It probably would have been easy to take him up on the job offer—well, kind-of offer. I'm not even sure he meant to offer me the job, since it was technically his son who'd made the initial suggestion. I just panicked and didn't want to be embarrassed or called a whore. Besides, I want things to be different for my boy, and that means I have to make better choices. I'll find a permanent job eventually, and then we can get an apartment, and it'll be a real home.

The man's eyes fall on me, and he stops. A slow, conniving smile spreads across his face, and it's so striking that I have to suck in a deep breath to center myself. He purses his lips and moves again, this time slower, more deliberate. As this nameless man moves toward me, his muscles tense and flex. His eyes darken, he licks his lips, and he smirks. I stand perfectly still, doing my best to pull my eyes from his. I can't. There's something about him that draws me to him. Maybe it's his commanding presence or the lust I feel when I look at him. This man is a goddamn disaster waiting to happen, I just know it.

"Just the woman I wanted to see," he said slowly. His eyes fall and travel up my body, a scowl forming on his face as he realizes his view is blocked. His expression changes from predator to protector. I don't know how I know that, but I do. Maybe it's something I see in myself, the change in expression. His dark eyes darken some, and a scowl forms. I'm just grateful to not see pity on his face. The moment a man's eyes go wide and he stares at me sadly is the moment I know it's all gone south. Love me, hate me, I don't care, but I don't want anyone's pity.

"Walked away the other day. Not cool, babe."

"Figured you were just being polite." I try to keep myself calm. This man unnerves me like no other. I just can't keep my shit together around him. *Jesus, woman, get it together*, I chide myself.

"I'm never polite," is his response. I don't doubt him, and if I'm being honest with myself, I know damn well he wasn't being polite the other day. I was just being awkward and didn't know what else to do, so I did what I do best—I ran.

"Okay then," I say and adjust my grip on Ian. My arms feel dead and my back aches, but my boy's body is tenser than it was when I picked him up, so I refuse to set him down now. Not until he's ready.

"The kid can't walk?"

"He can," I say carefully. I'd think after so many years of questions about my boy that I'd have a thicker skin by now. But I don't, and every judgmental comment just grates on my nerves. Just because he's quiet and he's far too big to be cuddled up in my arms like this doesn't mean he can't hear when people talk about it.

"Does he talk?"

"Excuse me?" My hackles are raised and my eyes have widened. I can't help the look that's on my face right now—a mix of frustration and anger—at the suggestion that my boy is slow. He's anything but.

He might be shy and, yeah, he doesn't talk a million miles an hour, but he's bright and capable and perfect.

"Jesus fuck, it was just a question, lady." He runs his hands through his hair, pulling at the ends, and blows out a deep breath.

"Not only can my boy walk and talk, but he can also hear the things you're saying about him."

Ryan's dad, whatever his stupid name is, throws his hands up in the air and backs his way out of the office, saying, "Whatever."

The doorbell chimes over the man's head, and when it stops, Ian squirms and I let him down. His eyes are still distant and his face is expressionless. As much as he likes me to carry him, he hates when people start asking questions. I could probably try to break him of the habit, but I'm too selfish to do so.

Robert, looking frazzled and nervous, wrings his hands together as he exits the office and approaches the counter. He puffs out his cheeks and stares at the cheap, outdated countertop before looking back up at me. I know this look. This is the look of disappointment and fear and regret. I've seen this look way more times than my twenty-five years should account for.

"Listen, Ruby. I can't have you doing this no more."

I knew it was coming, but it still stings. And it's sooner than expected to boot.

"Okay, um. Can we at least finish out the week with our arrangement? I have to buy my boy some new shoes, and I haven't been able to save anything yet. It's only been a week."

"Can't. Sorry."

As frustrated as I am with his suddenly short and rather dismissive attitude, I can't blame him. My problems are not his problems.

"Okay, um. Got any idea who's hiring in town?"

Robert's head cocks to the side in confusion, similar to the reaction I assume he'd give a naked woman, since I'm pretty sure Captain Comb-over's never seen a real set of boobs before. That's catty, but I don't even care. I just lost my not-super-sweet-but-still-better-than-what-I-had-before gig, and I got no other leads. So as far as things go, this whole situation sucks.

"Sweetheart, ain't nobody gonna hire you in

town. Not with Jim Stone running up in here like he just did."

"I'm sorry, what?" Now I'm the one staring at him in confusion.

"You might get a kick out of playing with fire, lady, but I sure don't. When Forsaken tells me I ain't supposed to be employing you, I listen." Robert pauses just long enough for my brain to start getting with the program. "Don't know what you did or why, but you got a target on your head. Jim Stone wants you for some reason, and if I were you, I'd go quietly."

"Is that his name?" I ask and point to the empty door to the lobby. Robert nods his head in confirmation. Jim Stone. He sounds like an ass.

"Ain't nobody in town gonna give you a job, Ruby. Jim's made sure of that. Best you can do is take the one he's offered."

My upper lip curls in disgust as I realize what he's saying. Here I am in a small town, in an isolated part of California, with nothing really near enough to get a job outside of town, and no car to take me there anyway. So much for starting fresh, free of the confines of club life. Jesus freaking Christ, this is perfect.

"I'll get the money for the room to you tomorrow, and I'll pay up for the week." I give Ian's arm a gentle tug, and we leave the lobby just as quickly as we entered. I'm fuming. My blood boils—okay, not literally—and my nerves are totally shot. I made the right choice—to get a job and stand on my own two feet. I took that first step toward independence and security and a life worth living. Something I could be proud to give my boy. But then Jim Stone happened and that all went to hell. Somewhere in the back of my mind, an excitement stirs in me. It's a ballsy move that I can almost respect. He's forced my hand, for some reason that's well beyond me, but at least I'll have some kind of job. It can't be worse than anything else I've endured to put food in my boy's belly. Or to keep him safe.

"Are we going to see the motorcycle club, Momma?" Ian's voice is louder than it's been in a while. Loud is good. Little boys are loud—that's normal. It's when he gets quiet that I worry.

"Yes, baby, we are," I say absentmindedly as we head down Main Street and trudge the few remaining blocks to Forsaken's clubhouse. I'm frustrated and mad at the very fact that this stupid man has just inserted himself into my business and made a decision for me without even asking if it's what I want. But there's also that niggling wonderment. I'd never admit it, not even to Ian, but sometimes it's nice to be saved. Not that I'm expecting a knight on shining chrome or anything, but it'd be nice if this guy turns out to be reasonably decent. I'm not expecting much, but he offered me a job when he didn't have to, and he's seeing to it that I take him up on his offer.

"Do you like this club?"

I think about his question a good block before answering. "I don't know yet. They seem like good people, yeah?"

"Yeah, maybe," he says. "Is Ryan going to be there?"

"I don't know, honey," I say. Truth be told, it's a weekday and too early for the school year to have ended, so he's probably at school right now. Like Ian should be. My heart sinks.

We walk up to Forsaken Custom Cycle with our pinkies linked together. The auto shop that sits in front of the clubhouse has a single garage bay open, and the office door is partially propped open with what looks like a brick. I'm still all sorts of angry and frustrated with Jim Stone, but now I'm equal parts nervous and on edge, too. Maybe he's not a bad guy, and this is a good thing.

No doubt sensing how tense I am, Ian smiles up at me says, "You got this, Momma." God, this boy. He makes me feel invincible and good. Like I'm not a total screwup.

"You lost, sweetheart?" A man who can't be older than thirty—or have showered in the last few days—walks out of the garage bay with his eyes trained on me.

"I'm looking for Jim Stone," I say firmly with my chin out and proud.

The man sizes me up from head to toe and back again. He's vaguely handsome in a way. Probably plenty handsome had I seen him before Jim Stone set his sights on me. As infuriated as I am with the man, I can't deny that I'm attracted to him. It's like I'm dead set on being attracted to the least desirable, most potentially-damaging man I can find.

"What do you want with him?" The man narrows his eyes, and it would intimidate me except for the fact that Jim's jet-black hair comes into view over the man's shoulder.

Raising an eyebrow, I smirk and say, "I guess he'll find out when I talk to him."

"I got it, Butch," Jim says, effectively dismissing him. The guy pauses a moment before he gives Jim a dark expression and stalks away. Once he's gone, I'm all too aware that I'm alone with Jim Stone now. He closes the distance between us, his bulking arms on display. I have to fight to remind myself that I'm annoyed with him. I'm flustered at the situation he's put me in, but above all, I'm terrified of what he's going to want me to do for him. I know nothing about this man or his club. I don't know a damn thing about this job he wants me to do.

"Say thank you." Jim's stupid-gorgeous gray eyes sparkle. I direct my attention from his eyes to his mouth, hoping I'll find that part of him less inviting, but it's a no-go. His lips are parted, and when he notices me looking, his tongue darts out, wetting them. I suck in a deep breath before regaining my composure and giving Ian's hand a reassuring squeeze.

"Is there a reason you're stopping me from feeding my boy?"

He's silent. Too silent and for too long. Ian takes a careful, slow step behind me and squeezes my hand back.

"Say thank you," he repeats. Now I'm sucking in a deep breath because his arrogance knows no bounds.

"Are you serious right now?" I shout, letting go of Ian's hand and closing the distance between me and Jim. I jab a finger toward my boy and step aside so the arrogant ass can see his face. "Look at my son. He's a little boy in a new town, and in case it's escaped you, he needs things like clothes and food and a roof over his head. All things I can't provide for him without a job. So how dare you bar me from getting a job in this town and then demand I thank you for the effort."

Jim grabs my arm and pulls me against him. I don't pull away, but I stay stock still and turn my face away, hoping he's not the kind of bastard who will hurt me in front of my kid. Jim's breath is hot and tangy against my cheek. Even though his grip on my arm doesn't hurt, I know all too well how that can change at any time.

"Let's get something straight, babe. You ain't got shit in this world except a kid who needs a whole lot more than he has right now, which is exactly why I made damn sure you won't find another job in this town. You might not like my methods, but everything I'm doing is to help you take care of that kid. From this point forward, you belong to Forsaken as long as you're in this town. You leave, you do so on your own—without the kid."

A mixed rush of anger and panic fills me and I push against him, but it does no good. Tears fill my eyes at the suggestion that he could take away my boy. I can't lose another kid. I won't watch another man take my child away. I'd rather die first.

"Stop fighting me and fucking listen," Jim says, his voice softer now. "I'm helping you. You work at the garage keeping shit straight and in the clubhouse keeping things clean. You're not here for sex, you won't be abused, and you won't lose your boy. You get on your feet and you want to leave, you can take him. But until you're stable enough to get him some real clothes and a place he can call home, you and that boy are under my protection and my supervision. You feel me?"

I can barely process what he's saying. He wants to help? People don't just do shit like that. There are always strings attached. Most clubs give their whores a little money here and there, depending on what they do for the club, but they don't employ them in the strictest sense of the word. I can't just ignore the repeated threats to take Ian from me, but I'm afraid I don't have a choice but to do as he says. In somebody else's life, this would be a godsend. In mine, it's how a nightmare begins. Jim's not the first man to offer me help to take care of my son. Ian will always wear the scars of that situation on his body for everybody to see. But mine? They're not visible— I'm the only one who knows they're there. No matter how much time passes, they'll always be there.

"Do I have another choice?"

"Don't like the deal, I already spelled the other choice out for you."

"Fine. When do I start?" My voice shakes with an anger and fear that brings me back to the last man who made me an offer I had no choice but to accept.

"Now. Trash bags on the bar," he says, hitching his thumb over his shoulder toward the clubhouse behind him. His other hand frees me from his grip, and he takes a few steps backward. "Place is a mess."

Before he can get too far away, I find myself wanting to say something to him, no, needing to say something. I might be his pawn right now, but that doesn't mean I have to be silent. My voice is steady and loud when I say, "Maybe you're just trying to help. Maybe not. But I won't ever forget that threat you just made."

CHAPTER SIX

June 1997

Sometimes, on days like today, I have to remind myself how much better my life is now. Three months ago, when Ian and I got to Fort Bragg, we had nothing but a suitcase and a backpack between the two of us. My boy had one pair of shoes. He had nightmares almost every night. Not just nightmares, but full-on night terrors that had him completely flipping out, screaming, and hurting himself. The six months before we got to California were undoubtedly some of the worst of his short little life. Before men who swore to protect us became the monsters that hunted us, Ian was a happy little boy who took our chaotic life with the ease of a child who knows nothing else. Afterward, he was nervous and on edge all the time. Even the times the clouds seemed to lift, he was still only a fraction of his old self. But now? In the last three months, I've seen more of who my boy used to be than ever before. And even though right now I'm ready to string him and his troublesome best friend up by their toes, I'm grateful for the life I have. Hell, I'm also grateful that Ian has a friend, much less a best friend.

I keep all these happy, sappy thoughts in mind as I carefully pull up to the elementary school in my borrowed minivan. It's a nice minivan, as far as minivans go, but it's not mine and so I'm driving like Miss Daisy. I don't actually know who it belongs to because Jim won't tell me. Not that we talk all that often. In the last three months, I've determined a few things about Jim Stone. He's not going to physically harm me. He meant what he said when he told me I wasn't going to be paid to have sex. He really is trying to help. Still, I don't know what his angle is. Nobody does something for nothing, and Forsaken's been doing a whole lot for me and my boy. When I got my first paycheck—or envelope full of money—I thought somebody had made a mistake. There was more than three times what I expected to find. After trying to ask Jim about it, he told me to talk to Ryan—his nine-year-old son—who's the one who told Jim he better pay me well. Two weeks later, Sylvia, Jim's mom, helped me find a little studio for me and Ian really close to the clubhouse. Despite the daggers the woman throws out of her eyeballs, she hasn't given me any trouble and she's good to my boy, treating him just like he was her own.

Ryan Stone. God, that kid is adorable. He's also a fucking handful, with a mouth that's made me blush a time or two and an attitude to match. Most days I can laugh it off, but this isn't one of those days. It's only the third day of summer school and I'm already getting a call to pick both boys up early. The lady on the phone didn't say anything except that there were behavioral issues. Which is just freaking perfect. Ian does not need to miss any school. As it is, I'm damn lucky Fort Bragg has a summer program to catch him up for the upcoming year. As long as he does everything that's asked of him and he scores high enough on his tests, they'll place him in the fourth grade, like he's supposed to be. Poor Ryan only got screwed into summer school because Jim got excited about free daycare. Not that the boy couldn't use some extra help. He's behind in writing and math but excels in reading.

Tentatively, I smooth down my hair and walk into the office. I almost forgot how brightly decorated elementary schools usually are. All in all, this seems to be a good one, not that I know a whole hell of a lot about it despite the fact that Ian's been to six different schools so far. I'm determined to make sure there's not a seventh. So when Jim Stone tells the school I can pick Ryan up and deal with his shit, I'm doing it. Even if the ridiculous little boy isn't mine, it looks like he's my responsibility for the day. I just hope his dad doesn't mind the fact that he's going to have to live by my rules, then.

"Can I help you?" Denise, the school's secretary, looks about middle-aged with only minor graying in her light brown hair. She has a friendly smile on her face, just like the two other times I've met her, and seems to really care about the kids.

"Yeah, I got a call to come pick up my kids." The words roll off my tongue before I even realize I've said them. Ryan's not mine—I know that. Sometimes it sure feels like it, though. With his dad coming in and out of the clubhouse at all hours, just leaving the kid there with me and Ian, I sometimes wonder if he even realizes his son exists. There's been no mention of a mother figure, and the only people I've ever seen take much time with the kid has been Sylvia and Jim.

Once in a while one of the members' old ladies will talk to him or give him a hug, but all in all, I think the boy is starved for affection. My hackles rise, remembering Jim's threat to take Ian away if I didn't get my shit together. The more I think on it, the more pissed off I become. There's more than one way to fuck a kid up, asshole.

"Their names?"

"Ian Buckley and Ryan Stone."

She hands me a clipboard to sign in. When I'm done, I set it down and wait while she makes a phone call. Barely any time passes before another lady, this one older and slower moving, comes out of a room and calls me over. I give Denise a friendly smile and beat back the dread that rises. I hate school administrators with a passion. Even the good ones are just too meddlesome for my liking. This lady seems nice enough. She introduces herself as Mrs. Marsh, and when she brings me into her office, I find Ian and Ryan sitting on opposite sides of the room, each facing a wall. Both turn their heads toward me just slightly. Ryan's nostrils flare and his bottom lip is jutted out, but there's a nervousness in his eyes when he catches sight of me. Ian looks my way, but his face remains passive, as if he's not really seeing me.

"Thank you for coming down, Mrs. Stone," she says and motions to a seat in the middle of the two troublesome little boys. Lord help me, she did not just call me that. Ryan's head jerks a little at the suggestion.

"Miss Buckley," I say. I almost explain to her that I'm not Ryan's mom or guardian, that I'm just his babysitter for the day, but I stop myself. For some reason, I don't feel like divulging all that business to her.

"Right. Miss Buckley, we had an incident today concerning bullying, and your sons' teacher felt it was serious enough to dismiss them from class early."

"What happened?"

"Ryan was overheard making fun of Ian on the playground and calling him names. When Ian began to cry, Ryan pushed him to the ground. The yard attendant tried to stop it, but Ryan completely ignored her."

Mrs. Marsh gives me a minute to process what she's just said. I have to close my eyes and take several deep breaths before I turn my eyes on Jim Stone's son, all the while reminding myself that he's a nine-year-old boy and not a fucking little demon.

Man, if it were legal to whoop his ass, I would.

"Do things like this happen at home?" There's the assumption again. I shouldn't have suggested Ryan's mine. He's not, and the school now seems to be under the impression that I'm with his father or something.

"No, they sure as hell don't," I say, with my eyes still boring holes into the back of Ryan's head. When he finally does turn to look at me, it's a very slow pivot. The steel of his jaw is betrayed by the water in his eyes.

"I have to say, Miss Buckley, that Ryan's always had behavioral problems. I reviewed his records before you got here. I also took a moment to review Ian's records, and I'm worried. This is not the first time Ryan's engaged in bullying behavior, and it likely won't be the last. With Ian's past—"

I don't let her finish.

"Stop right there," I warn coldly.

But she doesn't.

Because she's either stupid or prideful.

"With Ian's past, I'm not certain that this is a healthy situation for your son."

My eyes shoot first to Ian. All I can see beyond his mop of unruly dark blond hair is the single tear that falls down his cheek. My boy's sensitive, and he really hates when people talk about his past. I'd give anything to never have him shed another tear. Not that I have much to give, but I'd do anything for the adults of this world to understand that when they talk about kids in front of them, it fucks them up.

"Miss Buckley?" Mrs. Marsh's voice is quieter now as she draws me out of my thoughts.

"My son is fine," I say and lean over to run my fingers through his hair. His shoulders relax just a little from the contact. "He and Ryan have been friends for months now, and this is the first I've heard of any bullying."

"With all due respect, you're new in town. I've been principal of this school for over twenty years. Ryan's father was a student here, and he wasn't much better. Don't get me wrong. I don't think Jim Stone or his son are bad people. The boy needs discipline, a firm hand."

Ryan's body shifts in his corner. I lean toward him and give him the same gentle treatment I did Ian. Ryan jerks in surprise and curls in on himself, as if my touch hurt him somehow. This poor boy. What kind of punishment does he get at home? I'm not here as a representative for just my son, but Jim's as well. Which is something he and I are going to have to deal with later, but for now, I'm their advocates.

"I'll agree with you there. The kid has a smart mouth, and he gets away with murder, but that doesn't mean he's somehow unfit to be around my son. He's a nine-year-old boy." Suddenly, I find myself protective over Ryan. I never want him jerking away from me like that again. Damn it. This whole situation is pissing me off, and not just at Jim for abandoning his responsibilities as a parent to be here, but at the principal who's just trying to help, and at myself as well for ending up in this situation. I have no business telling another parent how to take care of their kid, but Jim's negligence rings fresh in my head. My boy may not have had much, but he's always had me regardless of how fucked things were, and I have to believe that's the most important thing a parent can give their child. As I sit here and look at Ryan, I wonder if Ryan feels that kind of love from anyone.

"Thank you for bringing this to my attention," I say and stand from my seat. Mrs. Marsh blanches with my unexpected dismissal of the issue at hand. I'm not undermining the severity of bullying, and I'm certainly not condoning that behavior toward my own son. But it's not lost on me that neither boy is going to talk right now, so sitting here hashing out where Jim and I have gone wrong with our kids isn't going to help find a solution for either boy.

"Miss Buckley," she says, standing quickly and smoothing down her pantsuit. I can see the questions in her eyes, but I'm done and I need to get these kids out of here before my insecurities bubble over and I totally lose my shit on this poor woman. Without giving her a chance to protest, I lean forward and offer her my hand. She blinks once before snapping to and clasping her hand in mine.

"Boys, stand up and thank Mrs. Marsh for dealing with your shit." I mentally give myself a good, hard kick for cursing in front of their principal. Probably not the best way to convince people that I'm a fit mother.

Ian moves first, turning his stoic face to his new principal, and in a small voice, he thanks her. I wait a beat for Ryan to move, but when he doesn't, I clear my throat and tap my foot on the floor as hard as I can. His black hair swivels around slowly, and his gorgeous gray eyes lift to mine. He looks like a puppy that's been whacked with a newspaper. I'd be lying if I said that I didn't like the look on him. I'm not callous, but the kid is a disrespectful little shit to most people. Except right now he's showing me respect. And that matters.

Reluctantly, Ryan mutters something akin to a thank-you as he stands up. The three of us leave the principal's office without another word. I walk a few feet ahead of the boys, not interested in coddling either of them right now. I hated being called into the office when I was in school, and I hate it no less now, but I especially hate being forced to defend and punish a child that's not mine. I could fall into this way too easily.

I could take responsibility for Ryan. I could teach him and love him and show him that some parents are sweet and gentle and kind. I could do it, and I want to, so much. But he's not mine. And deep down, I know why I'm so attached to him, why I feel the need to protect him. He won't ever replace the hole my twins left in my heart, but he does make it a little less painful. I don't think I realized how much focusing on other people helps ease my soul until I met this little boy.

We make it to the damn Donna Reed minivan before the boys start bickering. I'm so lost in my own thoughts that I don't even know who starts it, nor do I care. These kids are going to drive me to drink.

Pulling open the door to the back of the van, I turn to the boys and give them a damn mean glare to fit my mood. "Get this shit out of your systems now, because the moment we get to the clubhouse, I'm going to have bigger shit to deal with than this crap you two are pulling."

"The clubhouse?" Ian's voice is quiet as he asks the question. Ryan huffs and climbs into his seat. I take a deep breath and assure Ian that nobody is going to hurt him. He relaxes only a little, It breaks my heart that he has these fears, but I can't get into what happened at the school without Jim.

"My dad's gonna be really mad," Ryan says as well pull away from the school.

"I imagine he will be," I say, barely managing my own frustration at the whole thing.

CHAPTER SEVEN

The clubhouse is pretty empty this afternoon, despite the big party the lost girls are prepping for. When I left to go to the school, they were all discussing everything they needed to get at the store, so that's where they probably are right now. I can't say I'm not happy about having fewer people here to witness the shit storm I'm inviting on myself. It needs to happen, though. More than not wanting to get into a fight with Jim, I want him to take care of his kid. Ryan isn't my responsibility, and today is just one of the several times in the last few months that Jim's left me to parent his kid. And it has to stop.

Sylvia Stone, Jim's mother, sits at the bar with a

highball filled with a dark, caramel-colored liquid clutched in her shaking hand. Her eyes are downcast, but the telltale nod of her head tells me she's listening to the woman who's leaning over the bar top and whispering in her ear.

Ryan rushes into the room, shouting for his grandma and taking everyone's attention away from what they were doing. This is typical for Ryan. I'm not sure he's ever entered a room like a normal person. Sylvia pulls herself away from the other woman, who I only now recognize as Lona Phillips, one of the brother's old lady.

"You're home early," Sylvia says to Ryan with a raised brow. She lifts her eyes to mine. Her brow falls, and the expression on her face is none too pleased. Join the club, lady.

"Got in trouble. Grandma, you should have heard Ruby yell at my principal. She was awesome!"

"I didn't yell and it wasn't awesome," I say dismissively in Ryan's direction. Sylvia's face lifts just a bit, and I might be imagining things, but it's entirely possible she's giving me the world's smallest, most demure smile. I must be tired, though, because in the entire time Ian and I have been in Fort Bragg, Sylvia Stone has never so much as regarded me with any kind of thought, much less smiled at me.

"Is Jim here?"

"Is his bike outside?" Sylvia's mouth stretches in a firm line, but her blue-gray eyes shine in a way I've never seen before.

"That a yes or a no? I'm not in the mood for your shit right now."

Sylvia smiles with narrowed eyes. It's more predatory than I expect. Her lips quirk up and she preens, saying, "There she is."

"He's in his room," Lona says with a tight smile. Lona doesn't hang around the clubhouse much, but when she does, she always has her and Chief's daughter, Elle, with her. Ryan doesn't think I've noticed, but he's sporting a pretty big crush on Elle. She's a few years older than him and miles ahead in maturity, but it doesn't seem to matter to the kid. Sure enough, Elle rounds the corner with a pool cue in her hands. She taps her foot impatiently on the ground and stares at her mother. "You said you'd play with me."

"In a minute, baby."

"We'll play with you," Ryan says. He grabs Ian's

arm and drags him over to the unimpressed girl. To my surprise, Ian doesn't flinch or pull back. He just goes along with his friend. My jaw almost drops when I see a glint in my boy's eye that dances when Elle smiles at him. I let the sight warm my heart for just a moment before I force it down. I remind myself that I'm still pissed at Jim and can't have happy, fuzzy, mommy thoughts clouding my brain when I'm dealing with the way-too-sexy overgrown child. As it is, he has a way of distracting me from my purpose, and today I've vowed to myself that I won't be distracted.

Once the kids are off in the pool room, I excuse myself from Lona and Sylvia's presence and march across the room. The hallway off the main room of the clubhouse leads to the chapel—where the club's members have their meetings—and the pleasure palace, which is really no better than a seedy strip club but also houses six small bedrooms for the club's members to crash in when they need to. I know for a fact that one or two of them don't just crash in their room but keep it as their primary residence. Part of my job is cleaning not only the public areas of the clubhouse but the private areas as well. My least favorite part of the job is cleaning the bedrooms. I'm not stupid, so I don't talk about the things I find in there, but I can't say some of my findings don't make me look differently at some of the guys.

Especially Jim. When we first met, he was all suave and saying all the right things. Then he moved into the full-on flirting and casual mentions of how hot we'd be together. I've had more than a few rough nights of sleep after he'd dropped a comment like that, but the plethora of different-sized women's panties I've found in his room in combination with the dozens of condom wrappers gives me a damn good idea of what he's all about, and it definitely doesn't add up to the sweet nothings he tries to whisper in my ear. Jim Stone is a pig, plain and simple. Which I could handle if not for his incessant need to try to convince me he's not. I've fallen for that line of bull before, and I won't do it again. The price of being an idiot is way too high.

With an open palm, I slam my hands against the closed door to Jim's room. I don't even realize I'm banging until the door swings open and its occupants are glaring down at me. And they're pissed.

Jim's gray eyes are narrowed, and his bare, ripped chest heaves. Sweat collects on his brow and falls down his face. I suck in a deep breath and do my best to avoid thinking about how good he looks like that. Like he's run a marathon. Or fucked someone senseless. I don't have time to appreciate the view, though, because he has company, and she's damn intent on making sure I notice her.

"You need to wait your turn, sweetie." Condescension drips from every word that comes out of her swollen red lips. I'd call her on it, but I'm not convinced she's smart enough to understand it anyway.

"Maybe she wants to join us," Jim says. With a taunting smirk playing at his lips, he props himself up against the doorframe and lets his eyes roam over my body. Instinctively, my eyes fall to his chest and travel south. I don't want to look, but I do. And when my eyes find inches of skin below his navel, they keep going of their own volition. Tufts of jet-black hair protrude from between Jim's sculpted hip bones. His uncovered cock is out and proud. And pointing at me.

I gasp and snap my eyes up to his. I flush and stammer, totally failing at this whole being-unaffected thing I was going for.

"Yeah, she wants to join us." He snakes his hand out and tucks a loose strand of hair behind my ear. I move to pull back, but he's faster than I am and hooks me around the back of my neck, bringing me closer to him. I stumble over my own feet and land against his totally naked body. I try to push off of him, but he's got me now with both arms wrapped around my midsection. Anger flashes through me. How dare he answer the door naked? Even worse, how dare my body respond to his nakedness? Because that's the real problem here. Jim Stone isn't the first man I've seen naked. He's not even the first one to force his nakedness on me. No, the problem is that my hands are hot and damp, and the apex of my thighs isn't much better. My entire body is buzzing at the possibility of being with him.

And I hate myself for it.

"Let me go," I hiss. I don't care how my body feels about the situation. I spent way too many years listening to my body's demands and ignoring my brain's warnings. I have a little boy who's counting on me, and I won't disappoint him again.

Jim—who shall henceforth be known as King of the Assholes—leans in and runs his sweaty nose along my jaw. He sucks in a deep breath and holds it for a long moment before exhaling. And then he does it again. When I'm forced to breathe, all I can smell is sex and sweat. And her.

I have a choice to make. I could breathe him in

and let myself succumb to the nauseous feeling overtaking me at the woman's cheap perfume. I might get sick on him, but that would serve him right. Or—the more preferable option—I could force him to let me go.

As if reading my thoughts, he grins against my cheek and says, "Make me."

I could be beat for this.

I could lose my job.

I could lose everything I've fought so hard for.

But I don't give myself enough time to fully process how damaging this could be. My knee rears back as far as it can go before flying forward with as much force as I can manage. I make contact with bare flesh. Jim's response is immediate. He unhands me, and I take a few steps backward with my hands raised in front of me.

"Don't you ever touch me like that again." Something about the way he held me, and the suggestion that I'm nothing more than just a warm body for his personal pleasure, upsets me. I feel like a damn fool for ever thinking I might mean more to him than just an easy lay. I thought we were becoming friends or getting close enough that he'd see me as more than just a babysitter and a warm, wet hole. But I'm not, and once again I've just fallen for a line of bullshit, going so far as ignoring every red flag that's been waved in my face.

I've been a warm body before. I'm no better than the woman standing behind Jim, mouth agape and cussing me out. She's clutching a pillow to her front as if she's suddenly come down with a case of shyness. I've been her before. We all have to choose how to survive, and maybe being a lost girl is how she's managing to make it from sun up to sun down without throwing in the towel. I can't hate her for that, and I won't look down on her for it, either. But that doesn't mean I want to be her. It may only have been a few months ago that I was in her position, but those few months are important. They're the bridge between the woman who couldn't get anything right to the woman who's figuring out how to do right.

Jim's doubled over in front of me, gasping for breath. It's only a minute or so before he slowly rises to his full height. His face is red with a mix of anger and loss of breath, but his face looks better off than his poor dick. Not that he didn't deserve it, but maybe I didn't need to knee him that hard.

As I stare down this large, imposing man I see the guy I thought was becoming my friend. Jim Stone, despite being King of the Assholes, is the man who forced me to take a job that pays me well above what I should be making. He's the reason I have my apartment, even if I pretend he's not. My landlord let it slip that Jim bribed the man to give me the place for cheap without a security deposit. I suspect it was also Jim's doing that the apartment's appliances were upgraded right before we moved in. In hindsight, I probably should have weighed all this against his being an asshole before I decided to bruise his family jewels.

He takes a large step toward me and, instinctively, I step back. I want to believe he won't physically hurt me. I want to believe he won't fire me. But the reality is that it doesn't matter how nice he is or what he's done for me. He's Forsaken—an outlaw—and he makes his own laws and only follows the rules set forth by his club. He doesn't value kindness or forgive almost anything—his words not mine—and even if I want to think of us as friends, we're still virtual strangers. We don't talk much unless it has to do with work or the kids, and even then it's short and stilted. He almost always looks like he wants to say more but rarely ever does. And the times he does give himself more freedom to speak, it's to say something out of left field that I don't expect.

Like the time he told me he's never seen an ass fill out jeans the way mine does.

Or when he told me watching me clean makes his dick hard.

Or the time he wrapped his arms around me and rested his chin on my head and thanked me for being good to his boy. That almost killed me. It was quick and a small gesture, but it was so gentle and out of character from the man I'm used to seeing that I've carried it with me as a sign that Jim Stone is worth trusting my heart with.

But he's not, and this whole situation is proof of that fact.

So when he takes another step forward, I take another one back. We repeat this again and again until I'm moving so fast that I'm almost running backward as he stomps forward.

"What is your fucking problem?"

"Don't touch me like that!"

"Before that!" Now he's the one snapping and ill-tempered. Not that I can blame him. If I were him, I'd be pissed, too.

"What?" Now I'm confused and upset and afraid.

I'm a whole mix of emotions that I can't really place or explain. None of what I'm feeling makes much sense aside from the gnawing disappointment that's suffocating me.

"You banged on the door. You were pissed. Why?"

And in an instant, I'm back to being pissed about the whole thing at the school. Jim has this uncanny way of bringing me back to the present.

"You told the school I'd deal with Ryan."

"Yeah."

He cannot be fucking serious right now. That's his entire response? Yeah? No. No, that's not good enough.

Asshole.

"You put me in a really shitty position. Do you even know what the boys got in trouble for?"

"No, but I bet you're going to tell me."

My brain is about to implode from his lack of concern over his own kid. What is wrong with this man? The signs have been there for months, but I've been brushing them aside and trying to explain them away. Of all Jim's faults, this is the one I can't forgive.

"You put me in a bad position today, Jim! Ryan bullied Ian. Tell me how in the hell I'm supposed to handle that? I'm not Ryan's parent. You want me punishing him? Because that's not fucking fair. I should have been there to comfort my own kid, but instead I spent most of my time sitting in front of that goddamn principal defending both you and your son."

Jim's jaw ticks. His eyes darken. Every inch of him tenses. If I thought he was pissed about being kneed, I was wrong. No, now he's pissed.

"He did what?"

"You heard me," I say, throwing my hands up in the air and walking away. He doesn't seem to be up for parenting today, not that he ever seems up for the job, but I'm fucking done trying to force him to deal with this shit. I'll just take Ian home and find out from him what happened. We'll work out a way to deal with this on our own. I can't do anything about Ryan if his own father won't step up.

I'm well into the main room by the time Jim comes rounding the corner behind me. He's shouting

Ryan's name at the top of his lungs. I jump out of the way and let Jim pass. My hands shake at the sudden change in demeanor. Holy crap. Maybe Mrs. Marsh was right and Ryan's had a problem with bullying in the past. Maybe this is the straw that's breaking the camel's back of Jim's temper, because that's the only thing that can explain this sudden investment in a kid he largely ignores. For the millionth time since I've met the boy, I feel for him. Every kid needs a soft place to land, even if that soft place is a little screwed up. My heart breaks knowing that Ryan's softest place is with his grandmother, who isn't really that gentle with him.

As Jim disappears into the game room, I rush behind his increasing pace and do my best to ignore the men who now clutter up the main room. Even Rage, Jim's dad and the club's president, is in there. Rage doesn't like me, but he doesn't seem to dislike me, either. I'm half-convinced the only person on this planet he does like is his wife, and even that is tentative.

"You like picking on people smaller than you?" Jim shouts from the game room. I nearly fall over my own feet running after him. Once I'm able to tear my attention away from the curious onlookers, I'm thankful to find that Jim's at least slipped on a pair of loose fitted jeans so he's not exposing himself to everyone, including my poor kid.

Ian's wide brown eyes meet mine from across the room. They're filled with tears, and when he looks away, I gasp at what holds his attention. Jim's clutching Ryan, who's about a third his size, tightly on the back of his neck. Ryan's eyes are filled with tears, and he sucks in a pathetic little sob.

"Stop crying and tell me what you did."

"I, I—" Ryan stutters but doesn't actually make it past that before Jim squeezes his neck tighter.

I motion for Ian to come to me, but he's frozen in place, his eyes glued to the horrific scene before us. My feet and hands itch to pull Ryan away from his father. Jim's angry, angrier than I can explain, and definitely in no place to be talking to much less touching his kid.

"I'm fucking sick of you bullying other kids."

I can't pretend to know Ryan's history or what's causing Jim to snap like this, but it feels so extreme and way too intense. Ian doesn't have any bruises on his body, and he's walking fine. I'm upset that my boy's had a rough day, and I hate to think about Ryan treating my boy badly, but even I wasn't angry enough to be screaming at him. And it's my kid he was mean to.

"Jim, stop." I say.

He doesn't hear me, or he's effectively tuning me out, but either way, he keeps pinching Ryan's neck. Tears continue to stream down the boy's face, and Jim is in full-on bully mode. Watching the way he deals with his son's poor behavior gives me a damn good idea of where Ryan learned to bully people from. Christ, Jim can't expect Ryan to learn to peacefully resolve his issues if his father's first response to everything is to be a bully himself. I have to do something. I won't stand by and watch this boy be treated like this, and I don't care how much trouble it gets me in.

I rush forward and push Jim off of Ryan. Jim stumbles backward half a step, before righting himself. He's right on me, his chest pressing to mine. I have Ryan shoved behind my body. The boy buries his face in my back and uses my shirt as a tissue to dry his eyes.

Jim blinks in confusion as he stares down at me. He's not exactly scowling or glaring. The arch of his brows and parting of his lips is something else entirely. I just can't put my finger on what it is. He's still all wild and angry and frustrated. I don't know what to do with him right now, so I tread carefully.

"You were hurting him," I say in defense. "And you're scaring Ian."

Jim's eyes slide over to Ian, but the movement is uneven, like his brain is giving his body orders it can't quite follow. When his eyes come back to me, I signal for Ian to come to me, and this time, without Jim's angry eyes on him, he does. Ryan scoots over a few inches, and Ian joins him behind me. They're both so tall and yet so young at the same time. I can tell the difference between Ian's sure grip on the waistband of my jeans and Ryan's tentative one.

"You're high," I hiss.

"And you're beautiful." He reaches up and cups my chin in the palm of his hand. I keep myself still under his touch, refusing to lean into him. A couple years ago I might have been desperate or stupid enough to fall for his shit, but not now.

"Did you hear? They're making me VP, babe."

"Yeah, I know," I say. This is not the conversation I want to have. I want to yell at him for pawning his parental responsibilities off on me. I want to draw a line in the sand, telling him that I have my own shit to deal with. I don't need his, too. But this isn't the conversation we're having. He's seen to that.

"Then why are you mad?"

He's slowly slipping into madness. I've never seen Jim like this before, but he's taken something, and it's screwing with him big time. When I first got here, he was extra aggressive and pushy, and then he flew into that insane rage. Now he's slow to respond, and he doesn't even seem to remember why I'm angry with him. If I had the energy, I could strangle his stupid ass right now.

"The boys shouldn't see you like this," I say and take a step back. "I'm taking Ryan with me tonight. Get yourself cleaned up and be a fucking parent."

Still pressed against me, he doesn't move until I order him to. His unfocused eyes fight to make sense of what's going on around him, but when they can't, he takes a few steps back and stares at me in bewilderment.

I turn around to find Ryan with wide eyes, staring up at me like he can't believe I talked to his dad like that. I get the impression that no woman really talks to Jim like that. Well, maybe Sylvia should have taken a firmer hand with him before he was taller than her. If Ian grows up to be like that, so help me...

My boy's got his head bowed again, so instead of checking his mood, I just scoop him up in my arms and offer my hand to Ryan. He doesn't take it, though. Instead, the boy who's not really mine takes my pinky and gives it a squeeze. My heart clenches at the small but intimate gesture. He must have seen Ian holding my pinky like that at some point. It's not something he does often, but every now and then my boy opts for wrapping his entire hand around my pinky finger. I can't remember why he started doing it or when, but he does it when he needs a little extra care.

With my boys in tow, I walk us out of the clubhouse, completely ignoring the curious gazes from the looky loos at the bar.

CHAPTER EIGHT

"Okay," I say and lean forward conspiratorially. "So what happened at school today?"

The easy, light conversation falls away immediately, and I find myself the only party interested in this conversation. It has to happen, though. Ian's never been one to just come out with something that's been bugging him, so I'm not terribly surprised by the scowl he's giving the old wooden table that takes up the majority of our kitchenette.

"Well, dude. Out with it." My attention is now focused on Ryan, who's doing everything he can to avoid meeting my eyes. With Ian, this is all it takes to get him to open up. At least a little bit. He's not one to hold out when I ask him questions, so I'm not real used to sitting and waiting this long, but I do.

When I can come up with something to say to Ryan that might make him feel comfortable enough to talk to me, I break the silence and scoot closer to him. It dawns on me far too late that Ryan's probably used to being yelled at rather than spoken to, so I keep that in mind as I broach the subject again.

"Hey, you can talk to me. You're not in trouble, kid. But you do have to tell me what happened between you two."

"Nothing happened," Ryan says. It's way too quick for me to believe him, but I don't press. Instead, I wait it out and turn to my son, who's practically worn a hole in our table with his level on concentration. It's commendable how committed they are to keeping their silence, but I'm going to break them. If I can't break a couple of kids, I don't stand a chance when Ian's a teenager.

"Have it your way," I say and scoot my chair back. Just as I stand up, there's a loud, impatient knock on the front door. Both Ryan and Ian's eyes shoot up to the door. I give them a reassuring smile and cross the small room. Our apartment isn't much more than a kitchenette, bathroom, and a combination living and sleeping area. It might not be very big, but it's enough for us.

I press my eye to the peephole, surprised to find Sylvia Stone on the other side. Pulling the door open and moving aside, I dare not speak. I didn't really abduct her grandson, but I did leave with him. I already know she doesn't like me much, and after the scene in the clubhouse this afternoon, there's no telling where I stand with the club.

"Grandma!" Ryan shouts for his grandma and waves his arms in the air to get her attention. She gives him a smile and saunters into my apartment. Her eyes scan the room, her head bobs up and down, and she tosses her oversized purse on the couch. Sylvia's not a very tall woman, but she takes up space in a way I've never seen another woman do before.

"What are you boys up to?"

Neither of them answer Sylvia's question. Most likely because they're still keeping mum about what happened at school today. Which is what's important here. I do my best to ignore Sylvia's commanding presence in my small, private space, and I go back to what I was doing before she knocked on my front door.

"Do you like ice cream?" I open the freezer and cast Sylvia a sideways glance. She brushes her dark hair back from her eyes and nods once. Everything about this woman is so militant. She does what she has to and only says what the situation requires and nothing else. I try to follow her lead and do the same as I pull out two bowls and scoop some chocolate ice cream into each. I hand a bowl to Sylvia and grab spoons for each of us. She sits in the empty chair between the two boys and takes a bite of her ice cream while they stare up at her.

"Hey, I want ice cream, too," Ian says. Ryan pipes up complaining, but I ignore them as I take a few bites of my ice cream.

"I have something you want, and you have something I want. Think we can make a deal?"

Ryan's gray eyes narrow, and he folds his arms over his chest as he stares me down. Very slowly, I take another bite and smile down at the irate boy.

"Grandma, I want ice cream." With his attention now focused on his grandmother, his voice softens and his eyes are wide. Oh, well done, kid. He's trying to play her, but her lack of response tells me she's not buying it. I would have been surprised if she did, actually. I try to hide the smile on my face as she takes a bite of her ice cream and murmurs sounds of appreciation as she licks her spoon.

"You have until I finish my ice cream to tell me what happened," I say and take another bite. I'm mostly done now. Ryan eyes my bowl nervously as he shifts in his seat. After a few more minutes, he turns toward me.

"I'm not in trouble?"

"Nope. Whatever it is, you get a free pass this time." Whatever it is, I hope it's not so bad that I've made some kind of epic mistake by giving him a pass. Not that I can really do much of anything since he's not my kid, but I can stop doing the extras. I don't have to give him the approval he so desperately desires. I hate to take away something he needs, but it's literally the only leverage I have. Like all kids, he wants to be told he's good and worth being loved.

"Ian started crying. I wanted him to stop, but he wouldn't."

"Why was he crying?" A lump forms in my throat, making it hard for me to speak, but I manage. I should be used to it by now—the intense gut reaction that happens when my boy is hurting—but I'm not. And I'm starting to think I never will.

"I don't know. I didn't do anything."

Turning to my son, I reach out and place a hand on his arm gently. Ian's eyes lift to mine before they slide over to Sylvia. She gives him a soft smile. Most of the tension seems to leave his body at the small gesture.

"What happened, baby?"

"Jenny touched my face."

"And you started crying?"

Ian nods his head but doesn't look my way. Instead, his eyes fall on Ryan, who's looking right back at him.

"What happened next?" Sylvia's eyes are on me as I ask the question. Her gaze seems to have softened some. The more time I spend around Sylvia, the less I see her harsh lines and disapproval, and the more I see a woman hardened by life. She looks tired and rundown. She's old enough to be my mother, but when I look at her, I have to wonder if I look as haggard. Most days, I'm grateful for even a moment's relief. A single breath where I don't worry about my son or if I'm going to lose my job and be out on my ass again. An hour where I'm not terrified of all the good that we're getting because we've had so much bad that I can't quite believe the good will last. What I would give to not live in fear every single day...

"Answer her," Sylvia says, eyeing Ryan. I have to shake away my thoughts so I can refocus. It's getting late, and I have yet to get any answers.

"Jenny made him cry, so I told her not to do that."

"And?" As I wait for the rest of the story—because there must be more to it—I fix the boys each a bowl of ice cream and hold them ransom until they get to the damn point already. It's not the big things that exhaust me as a mom. It's the little moments like this where I can't just ask a question and get a straight answer. Everything is a production with kids.

"I pushed her," Ryan says. He's barely noted the bowls in my hands. Instead, his eyes are on mine. There's a kind of desperate need in his gaze that makes me want to reach out and hug him. And I probably would if his grandmother weren't right here. But she is. Ryan is her boy, not mine. I can barely take care of my own son, let alone someone else's. Not to mention everything I've lost that I don't dare mention.

I hate the idea of a kid Ryan's size pushing a girl, but I nod my head to urge him to keep going. He's talking to me, and that's a sign of trust that I value.

"Ian got mad at me for pushing her. I was only trying to help. He was being stupid."

I stifle a yawn and hand the bowls to the boys. I'm too tired for any more of a play by play. Especially with Sylvia sitting here, watching me deal with this. So I run through all the shit I'm obligated to know as an adult in charge, like asking if Jenny is smaller than they are, and asking Ryan if he understands why pushing other people—especially people smaller than him—is wrong. They yawn and get grouchy as they try to respond. A few times I have to snap my fingers to get Ian's attention. The poor kid is half-asleep since it's already a solid hour after his bedtime. That's new, the bedtime thing. He used to have one a long time ago, but it kind of fell off with all the moving and chaos we were living in every day. Now that we have some sense of normalcy, I'm pretty rigid about bedtime, but this was a strange day.

I've already put my ass on the line for Ryan once today, but I'm about to do it again, whether his grandmother is watching or not.

"You don't like it when your dad is mean to you, do you?"

To my surprise, Sylvia doesn't react. Ryan's sideways glance at her is telling. He doesn't want to get in trouble, but her non-reaction seems to ease him a little, and he shakes his head.

"And he's a lot bigger than you, isn't he? He's bigger just like you're bigger than Jenny. I want you to think about how that makes her feel the next time you decide to be mean to someone. I don't think Jenny was trying to upset Ian, and as much as I like the fact that you defended him, I don't like that you pushed her."

"I'm sorry," he says. His big gray eyes shine up at me. My heart warms, and for the first time since we started this conversation, I don't feel the slightest bit awkward about disciplining someone else's kid.

"Okay, time for bed." I instruct Ian to take Ryan and get some pajamas on and to go crawl into bed.

Sylvia and I sit in silence at the kitchen table while the boys get ready to go to sleep. Ian tells Ryan he has to brush his teeth, but the kid doesn't have a toothbrush here. I turn away when Ian hands his over and Ryan starts brushing. I think I'm supposed to tell them they shouldn't share or something, but I'd rather they both have clean teeth when they go to bed, so I don't say anything. Thinking about where Ian and I were last year, hell even four months ago, I find myself stunned to silence. I didn't have the luxury of worrying about clean teeth before. I was just lucky he was eating, or he was aware enough that I could talk to him. His night tremors are almost a thing of the past now, and my boy eats like a miniature horse. I was able to get him into the doctor, and he's finally back to normal weight for his height and age. I stood there—in front of the doctor, her nurse, and my boy—and I fucking bawled. I felt such incredible relief and gratitude that he was healthy, I couldn't control my reaction. I didn't even apologize for it, either.

"You're good for them," Sylvia says.

I blink at her, not knowing what to say. Diverting my eyes, I see the boys are already passed out in bed. Unfazed by my response, she just smiles all-knowingly, and I have to admit it's creepy as fuck. Until now, I felt like the woman barely noticed me, but now, as I sit at this table with her, it feels like she's paid a hell of a lot better attention than I thought.

"My son likes you, but he's an idiot. I don't know

that he deserves you, but I know damn well that my grandson does. I've never been good about giving Ryan gentle. I guess I wasn't gentle with Jim, either. I let his dad convince me that boys need to be commanded, not coddled."

"I think you can do both," I say quietly.

"I think you can, too. In fact, I'm counting on it. I'm not going to be here forever."

"I'm not... trying to be Ryan's mother, but I also can't just watch Jim bully him like that."

"And that's why you're good for them. Not many men stand up to my son, let alone women. Jim needs a woman he respects, and he respects you. I wasn't sure why at first. But I've been watching you, Ruby Buckley. You've done a lot with very little, and I respect that. So does Jim. I'm not here because you're good for Jim. Or Ryan. Even though you are. I'm here because I know that if you give him the chance, he'll be good for you, too. I see you with your boy. You hover—obsess—over him. You're giving Ian what I should have given Jim and never have been able to give Ryan."

"Why are you telling me this?" It's not what I want to say. I want to ask her why she thinks I'm good for Jim or something equally as flattering. I want to know what she sees that I don't.

"Cancer. They're taking my tits."

"I'm sorry." It's not enough, but it's all I have. I've never really been around somebody with cancer before, so I don't know what to say or how to be supportive. Fuck. I suck at this shit.

"I'm not here for sympathy. You know what's happening tonight. Why aren't you at the clubhouse?"

"After this afternoon? Hell no."

"He wanted you there. It's a big day for him." Sylvia leans back and turns toward the boys. A smile finds its way to her lips before it falls. "Ryan was three months old when CPS dropped him off at our house. Jim had to grow up quick, just like I'm sure you did. My grandbaby's never had a mom—until now."

I wipe my sweaty palms on my jeans and focus on the small but inane act with more attention than is necessary.

"Go. I'll watch the boys."

"I shouldn't," I say. I want to. God, I want to.

Part of the reason I was so grouchy about having to pick the boys up early is that I wasn't able to help prep the clubhouse for Jim's party. The club's old president just retired to their mother charter in Nevada. Rage went from VP to President last week, and now they've made Jim their new VP. This night was important to him. He talked about it for over a week. And I know he wanted me to be there. But he was high today. And mean. He wasn't just an asshole. Jim was something I've never seen him as before, and it scared me. I want the guy I was getting to know, who treated me like a person, back. I want the guy who I thought was my friend, not the man who showed up today.

"Go," she says, more urgently this time. "You're more than a mother. Go be a woman for a change."

I don't hesitate or think twice about my decision. I just... go.

The clubhouse is only a few blocks over, so the walk isn't long. If anything, the cool summer air is refreshing. You'd think it'd bring me to my senses, but it doesn't. The salty tones from the ocean and the crispness from the evening's rain wakes me up in a way I'm not sure I've been in months, if not years. I doubt Sylvia Stone shows up to play babysitter for just anyone, and I'm even more doubtful that she lets herself be vulnerable in front of people she doesn't trust. If she trusts me enough with her confessions, then I should trust her enough to let myself believe that maybe life is getting better, that maybe Jim isn't just the bastard he was being this afternoon. Maybe, if I can be a good mother now even if I wasn't then, then perhaps it's possible for Jim to be a good man, too.

Inside the gates of the clubhouse, there are three metal barrels filled with God-only-knows what and set ablaze. The outside lights shine bright. The lot is free of people, but a large crowd roars and swells beyond the tall, chain-link fence. I've never seen people back there before, much less so many. Fort Bragg sits directly on the coast, with much of its shoreline high above the Pacific. The clubhouse sits a few hundred feet from the edge, on land that once belonged to the US government but was long-ago parceled off for pennies on the dollar. Jim once told me there was only one reason Forsaken ever crossed that fence line and it's for something he hopes he never has to witness. It's stupid, considering the excited roars from the crowd, but still, I pause before I push my way through the gate in the chain-link. I've been in town for months, but even with my tentative friendship with Jim, and working for the club, I still feel like an outsider. I'm not a member or family or even somebody's woman. And Jim's made damn sure nobody touches me, so I'm not a lost girl, either. I'm just...me. And here I am, at this party that's a big deal for Forsaken. But I push on because, despite feeling out of place, I can't bring myself to turn back now.

You're good for them.

The cheering is loud at the edge of the crowd, but in the middle of it, it's deafening.

Forsaken from different charters hold up cans of beer in victory, shouting at the men in the center of the ring. Men and women in plain clothes crowd around the brothers, their excitement no less apparent.

An older Forsaken from Nevada leans into the man next to him, who I automatically recognize as Rage, Jim's father. "Ten bucks says your new VP hits the ground before he can get another punch in."

Rage snorts his reply and puffs his chest out. I peer up at him with narrowed eyes. He takes note of me immediately but doesn't soften in my presence. With his eyes locked on mine and words meant more for me than the man he's addressing, Rage says, "If he can't handle fresh meat, then he hasn't earned the right to wear the patch." I find myself harboring a not-so-deep-seated hatred for Jim's father. No wonder Jim doesn't know how to show Ryan much softness—he sure as hell didn't get any from his own father. Sylvia's confession rings in my head as my mouth runs away with me.

"If your VP can't hack it, maybe his president can't either," I say and push my way through the crowd before Rage can show me how he got his nickname. I know he's a mean old bastard, and I've seen enough of him to know better than to ever mouth off to him again.

"Hey, Psycho," a familiar voice shouts from nearby. My head shoots up as I make it to the edge of the ring to find Butch eyeing me with a knowing smile. "Your girl's here."

The two men in the center of the ring turn in my direction, making me gasp. Standing just a few feet away from me is Grady, the newest patched member. One of his arms hangs limply by his side, and his lip is busted open. He wobbles in place but manages to right himself before falling over. Grady looks like shit, but it's Jim's appearance that makes my blood run cold. One of his eyes is swollen shut. His nose is bloody, and he stands awkwardly, favoring one leg. I move toward him without even thinking. These men have been fighting. They're jacked up on adrenaline and masculine pride. Jim's standing depends on him winning this fight, and Grady's young, but he's got a lot to prove to his brothers. He's also built like a damn semi and is a decade younger than Jim.

Grady's woman, Layla, walks into the ring and brings him a beer. With his attention focused on her for the moment, I take a few steps toward Jim before stopping.

Jim focuses on me with his good eye and smirks. He raises one arm and points in my direction. The smile that takes over his face is infectious. He crooks a finger my way, and I burst into the most ridiculous smile. It feels like an out of body experience or something. My entire body is buzzing, and there's this heavy thudding in my chest. My face is flushed, and my palms are damp. Everything about this moment feels right and amazing and something that I don't hardly deserve.

I rush to Jim and throw myself into his arms only to realize how injured he is. I have to pull Jim upright before he topples over.

"Careful, Momma," Jim purrs into my ear. His voice is silky smooth and totally devoid of the crazed undertones it had earlier. This is all Jim. This is the guy who loans me a fucking minivan so I can get my son to and from school—even if I've somehow ended up taking his son, too—and he pays me well above what I should earn just so I can feed my boy and give him normal. This man looks at me in a way that makes me feel like maybe I'm worth something after all.

"Kiss me for good luck," he says, leaning in. Jim takes a deep breath and tries to suppress a groan.

"You're in pain." I twist just enough to eye him warily. I don't want to hurt him any more than he's already hurting, but damn if the prospect of kissing him doesn't have my stomach doing flips.

"Been in pain since I met you, Momma. Every day I'm working a plan to make you mine."

A million things run through my mind at once. He's insane. He's saying the exact right things. He's also drunk, that much is evident from the scent of whiskey and beer on his breath. But he's still Jim. I'd convince myself it was the alcohol talking if he were pulling some cheesy one-liners on me, but he's not. Maybe I'm stupid, but this feels genuine. So I ignore every ridiculous thought that's running through my head and gently press my lips to his, careful not to hurt him any more than he already is. Jim's kiss is gentle but firm. And holy fuck, my body is awake and alight.

In an instant, I feel like I've found my way home and been submerged under water at the same time. I don't think I've been lonely, but kissing Jim makes me feel like I've been missing a big part of me that I didn't even realize wasn't there. My heart thuds and my stomach acts up again, but this is right. We're right. And even if I can't have him right now, and he's still an asshole and I'm still a disaster, I want us.

I just hope I'm not falling down the rabbit hole never to return.

CHAPTER NINE

Jim
Brooklyn, New York
April 2016
Mancuso's downfall

Everything hurts. Except my heart. It's cheesy as fuck and dumb as hell, but it's true. I fight through the pain just to look at her. Sometimes it's so bad that my vision fades. It's just for a moment, though. I can handle the pain, but I can't handle losing her.

"What's with the tears, baby?" I try to keep my voice playful, but even I can hear how feeble I sound.

"Just looking at the hottest piece of ass I've ever seen," Ruby says with a sadness to her voice that I wish I didn't recognize. She hovers over me, her hair pushed back over her shoulders and her clothes soaked in blood. My blood. It's not fucking right. I promised her that nothing would ever touch her. I told her I'd keep her and her kids safe, and then I bring this on her? A hoarse, angry laugh escapes me.

Five good things have happened to me in my life. The first was Ryan, even though I've never told him that. I should tell him... just in case. The second was Ruby. My woman, God, my fucking woman. I didn't know how to be a dad, much less a man, before I met her. I didn't know why my father put up with my mother's bullshit or why she put up with him at all. I didn't understand any of it until I met Ruby. And then it was like everything clicked in fucking place. I didn't have a death wish before, but I sure as fuck didn't know what it meant to live, either.

The other three good things are my other children. First it was Ian. Ruby tells me he needed me, but she's wrong. I needed him. I needed the boy who screamed in his sleep, who couldn't defend himself, and who clung to his momma like his life depended on it. I needed that boy—I still need him—in ways I can't even explain. And the twins.

Fuck, the twins. We don't talk about it because we're men and we're Forsaken. And we don't need to. But my middle son and I are the same. Neither of us could let ourselves get close to Alex when she first came to town, because we already loved her too much to let her like us and then eventually hate us. With Michael, it's easier. He has a fire in him that's so much like the man Ruby used to know, it scares me when she makes those confessions. Michael has it in him to lead his family. He knows that men who live outside the bounds of society don't always have the luxury of being good men, but rather they often have to force themselves to merely live with their life's choices. But that's not Alex. She's our hopeless optimist—so much like her mother in that way—that she believes she can live in darkness and still love in the light. No man ever recovers from loving a woman who hates him, and so we tried in our own ways. Ian kept his distance, and I channeled my fear, and we pushed her away. And because she's more Ruby than she is Mike, she pushed her way through it without ever losing herself.

"Jim, baby!" Ruby's panicked screams bring me to, and I force a smile to my face. At least I think it's a smile. Everything is so fuzzy, and I'm being moved and jostled, and I can't really focus on her. But I feel her skin on mine, and I know her hand is griping mine tight. I can't feel how tight she's holding on, but I can see the whites of her knuckles. My arm is weak, and my hand is numb, I think. But muscle memory allows me to remember how to squeeze her hand and show her that everything is okay. Because it has to be. Almost twenty years later and she finally has everything she needs to be whole, and I won't let her hurt for a moment, not even over me.

Somewhere in the background, I hear faint sobbing. I try to focus on it. We're in the van. There's so much movement, but the pain is subsiding, so that's a good thing, I think. I close my eyes and listen to the world around me. It's not Ruby crying—it's my son. Ryan. He's somewhere in front of me and he's crying. My kid who rarely ever cried as a child and is essentially allergic to feeling as an adult is in tears. And somewhere, in the back of my mind, I know he's not crying over me.

I open my eyes and will myself to see what's going on around me. Ian and Mindy are crowded around Ruby, and they're all staring down at me, holding me, supporting me. They're focused on me, but Ryan is focused on something else. There's only one thing on this entire fucking planet he could be this upset over. And that thought makes my blood run cold.

"Don't," Ruby warns. Her soft voice is gone, and in its place is the tone she uses when I'm about to suffer for a good long time over being stupid. This is her mom voice, and even though I'm her husband and not her child, I still feel like I'm about to be sent to the corner. I don't listen, though, because she's in mom mode as much as I'm in dad mode, and my boy is crying over my girl, and I'm not going to fucking lay here and pretend like that's not more important than listening to my wife.

So I move to sit up. It hurts, and my side aches and is somehow also kind of numb. Nothing feels real, and yet every movement is topped off with another sharp pain that radiates from somewhere near my ribs. Blood tickles my side as it seeps from my wound. It's such a weird feeling—knowing I've been stabbed and not really feeling it the way I think I should—especially when I've been stabbed before. This is just... different.

"He's fine," Ruby says, as if reading my mind. She's blocking my view of our son and daughter, and I know damn well it's intentional.

"Don't fucking lie to me!"

Ian is behind me now, holding me upright. He nods his head at his mother. I lose sight of them for a moment before I remind myself what I'm fighting to stay coherent for—my family. They'll survive without me, but I'll be damned if they lose me in this fucking van.

"Ma," Ian says in a harsh tone.

Ruby, in all her ever-loving stubbornness, doesn't move.

"Mike cut her pretty bad, baby. You don't need to see it."

"I'm not a fucking child. Now, move," I order her. I've got a hole in my fucking side and she's trying to baby me while our daughter is hurt. Why the fuck is she here with me and not with Alex?

"If you try to move, I will knock you out myself," she says in response.

But then she moves, and suddenly I know why she didn't want me to see this. I know why she was hesitant to let me look at our girl with her face all sliced up and blood covering both her and Ryan. I know why she didn't want me to see our daughter's blood covering our son and the tears that streak his face. Because I cry out, so loud, so fierce, and with such anger that I jerk forward and immediately regret it. My wound throbs and aches in a way I can't even describe. Everything goes black, and I hear voices around me, people talking in hushed tones, or maybe they're screaming. I can't tell. But they're freaking out and asking each other how long until we get to the hospital, and it's so chaotic, but all I can see is Alex's face in my mind. Her beautiful face that once was flawless is now carved up with scars identical to the ones Mike gave Ian. And I hold on to that image for as long as I can. I let myself stew on it to the sounds of my son crying, and I take it all in. Because never in my life have I ever felt the kind of hate and anger I do now. Never have I been more resolved to survive something. Carlo Mancuso has taken one too many things from my family, and he is a fucking dead man.

CHAPTER TEN

Ruby
Fort Bragg, California
July 1997

"I'm gonna go clean up the rooms," I say to Layla, Grady's wife. She's had her ass perched at the bar for over an hour now and hasn't said much of anything after I pissed her off. She needed to hear what I had to say, so she can just get over her shit. Babies deserve a mother who puts them first and fuck her for not putting all that shit aside for her baby.

Speaking of people getting over their shit…

It's been over a month since Jim was patched in as VP. He's always been an asshole, but lately it's like he's competing in the asshole Olympics. The first couple of weeks, he'd probably have won bronze. But after yesterday? That motherfucker is a damn gold medalist. He makes my head spin with his mood swings. One minute he's smiling and flirting with me and the next he's shutting down and is acting cold as ice. I can't make sense of it, and I'm done trying to. We spent months volleying between snipping at one another and flirting. Then we kissed and it was romantic and all this stuff that I never thought I'd get. But because my life's a bitch, I never did really get it. We kissed, and Jim finished his fight with Grady—he won—and then he got absolutely shit-faced with the boys. And I had to leave to take care of our kids. I don't know what I expected, but I expected a hell of a lot more than I got. That night just confirmed what I already knew, but stupidly let myself forget. Anything I might be feeling for Jim is just that—a feeling—and it can't be anything more.

"Do what you want," Layla says with a coolness that's only there to mask her anger. Biting my tongue, I ignore her and walk away. Dumb bitch is pregnant but won't put the drugs away long enough to make sure her kid is born with half a brain. To say I hate her might be an understatement.

I start with the pleasure palace—because it's my least favorite room—and work my way back toward the main room. I skip over Jim's room long enough to finish the rest of them before I finally buck up enough to take care of it. The pleasure palace is my least favorite because of the sheer volume of gross going on in there, but Jim's room is the most difficult. It doesn't look any different from the other rooms when I first walk into it, and it's no bigger than any other room either. He's not messier than his brothers and it's not like it gets cleaned so seldomly that I find moldy food or dead rodents under the bed. It's just… the room smells like him. And when I open the door, it's the first thing I'm hit with. His scent. This intoxicating mix of leather and tobacco that's just subtle enough that the smell of his soap overrides it. There are only two rooms in the clubhouse that have their own bathrooms, and Jim's is one of them. He's been using this small room and attached bath as his home for a few weeks now. I don't even know when it started, but he's just kind of stopped going to his house. And I've had Ryan with me and Ian.

Silvia knows, and she's offered to take Ryan on her good days. If I'm being honest with myself, I don't let her because I want him with me, not because I'm worried about how much she can handle right now. It doesn't really matter though, because I think she knows. Ian is my son and I love him in ways I don't have words for. My loving Ryan doesn't take away from that love, it only adds to it. When Ryan's around, I see my little boy—not this shell that he was before we moved here—and for that alone I love that boy. But I also love his smile and his laugh. I love his heart and the way he seeks me out. I love the way he makes me feel needed and wanted and important. Ian's the only other person who's ever made me feel like this. So even though I'm tired and I want Jim to step up and be a damn parent, I also don't want to lose my boy. I don't relish the day I have to face the fact that Ryan isn't mine and no amount of playing mommy is going to make up for that fact.

Before I know it, Jim's bathroom is clean. None of the typical signs of life were on the floor or in his wastebasket. Signs of life being condom wrappers and random pieces of underwear. Jim chases me for months, acts like he's my friend, and then lets me clean up his fucking condom wrappers. When he first told me he can't remember Ryan's mother, I was surprised. Not that I remember a whole hell of a lot about Ian's father, but that's on him, not me. Asshole didn't even wait until the stick turned blue to cut bait. Maybe it was less about surprise that a man could have a kid with somebody he can't remember—not that it matters since she's dead—but more that Jim, my friend, a guy I thought was a decent person, couldn't remember a woman who'd supposedly told him she was having his baby.

"Men. Fucking pigs—the whole lot of 'em," I walk back into the bedroom, muttering to myself, with the garbage bag in hand and contemplate whether or not to toss the pile of dirty clothes from the floor into the bag. My grandpa had a rule about that shit growing up. You put your clothes away. They end up on his floor and he'd chuck 'em. Didn't matter what they were. It's tempting, but I have enough shit to work out with Jim to add that infraction to the list.

"What's wrong, Momma?" Jim's deep voice sounds curious, not worried. But I'm screaming from the shock of it. I thought I was alone. My right hand grips the half-full trash bag as I swing it out in front of me. My left just flies around maniacally. Only when I come to the realization that I'm screaming like a banshee do I come to my damn senses and shut myself up. Comfortably stretched out on the bed is Jim. His jet black hair is tucked behind his ears and his gray eyes dance as he smiles up at me.

"I hope you're better at defense when you're

home with our boys."

Our boys?

I don't put a voice to the words that fly through my head, but I know damn well that my face is saying it for me. He has got to be fucking kidding me. I struggle every single day to be a decent mother to my own kid and because Jim can't step up and be a fucking father, I've got Ryan too. And he has the nerve to suggest that I can't take care of those boys on my own? Hell no and fuck that and fuck him, too.

And because this man makes me lose my marbles and doesn't even have the courtesy to patronize me a little, I let out another scream and throw the bag of trash at him. I don't run, which is really what I should be doing right now. MC's are all the same. The club is about brotherhood and the brotherhood is about pride and respect. Even though the guys try to turn the bullshit off with their women in private, they never fully do. Those patches and that ink becomes who they are, whether they like it or not. Jim would find me quickly, but at least I'd have a head start before I had to deal with the consequences of my actions. Because there are always consequences.

Always.

But I don't run because I promised myself I'm going to do different, better even, than before. I told Ian that we're home now, and I meant it. So I dig my heels in, chest heaving, eyes narrowed, and I dare Jim to say a word to me.

And because he's fucking stupid, he does.

Roaring up off the bed, he's in my face in a matter of moments. With our height difference, he bends at his knees to meet my eyes. His stubbled jaw is locked in place. And we stand like this, each about ready to clock the other, in total silence. I'm pretty sure if I speak right now, it'll be to tell him to go fuck himself, and he'd probably be saying much the same thing to me.

The last few weeks Jim's been even more distant and the soft and flirty thing he does has been fewer and further between. I should be grateful that this is my biggest issue in life. My boy and I have a home, he even has a regular pediatrician, and he's fucking killing it in summer school. We read every night and work on our math and vocab words every afternoon. Ryan's doing good, too, but he's such a pain in the ass about doing his homework. At this point, I'm just glad I've managed to find ways to get him to do it. It was touch and go for a couple of weeks there, but once I figured out his vulnerabilities, I've been able to exploit them. Which is another thing—my kid has friends. As in plural, as in holy shit, my poor, sweet little boy plays with other kids and he smiles and he fucking laughs. Jim doesn't get why that hits me so hard. He told me I was overreacting, but Silvia got it. She doesn't know Ian's history—nobody here does—but she's a mother. She doesn't have to know my boy's damage to appreciate my happiness over something so small. She's not doing great these days, but she hides it well in front of the boys. I give her what support I can, but Silvia Stone is not one to accept help no matter how much she needs it.

"Well, you gonna stand there all day or are you gonna yell? I got shit to do," I say. In the time it's taken my mind to wander over how much worse my situation could be, he's stood stock still and just stared at me. His eyes are at first blazing hot and crinkled in the corners, like he's angry; but then he's just kind of spaced out from the looks of it. Which might actually be worse because I can't figure out what he's thinking.

And he doesn't tell me. Instead, he reaches out and cups my face in his hands and pulls me in. In a rush, his lips are on mine and they feel damn good. All soft and velvety and... like bubble gum. Only, he's not chewing bubble gum. I straighten my back and try to pull away, but he won't let me, and fuck him for this shit. What an asshole. Jim's lips are never this soft and he damn sure doesn't go around chewing bubble gum. Without another option, I reach up, and place my hands on his chest. And I bite down on his lower hip. Hard.

He pushes himself off me, sending me back into the door frame. Pain radiates from the back of my skull, but it doesn't matter. The quick rise and fall of his chest in partnership with the narrowing of his eyes is all the satisfaction I need.

"You stupid bitch," he hisses. For the first time since I got to know him, a sliver of genuine fear runs through me. Jim won't hit me, I tell myself. He's not like the rest of them. But he takes a step forward, and it's so slow and calculated that I recognize it for what it is. He won't hit me, I promise myself. Another step and he's almost on me. But he might. Because that's what men do—even good men.

"Stop." The word leaves my mouth as something between a command and a panicked shout.

"You're going to pay for that."

I put up shaking hands and take a deep breath. I say it again when he doesn't listen, but my voice breaks under the effort. My hands clench into balls at my sides as my lungs strain for breath. Jim's black hair lightens to the darkest brown I've ever seen. It's no longer a windswept mess around his face and is slicked back with an expensive mouse that keeps it set. His pale skin darkens and takes on an olive complexion that is purely Mediterranean. Gray eyes darken to a deep brown and the man before me grows a few inches. It's no longer Jim Stone, my infuriating friend, who stood before me moments ago is no longer. In his place, is Carlo Mancuso. Mike when I knew him. And his lip is curled, his voice spitting venom, and he's holding my six-year-old son to him with a knife to my boy's throat. I try to shake it away, knowing it's just an illusion, but it feels so real. Short pulls of breath are all I can take in, they're not nearly enough to keep the pressure from swimming in my head. My eyes fall closed as I try to regain control of my mind and body. I can barely think clearly enough to suck what little air I can into my lungs. It's just... my throat is so tight. This doesn't make sense. None of it makes sense.

Jim says my name, but it sounds like he's far away, and his voice still carries a thick New York accent. I reach out, but lose my balance. No sooner than I'm falling forward is Jim catching me in his arms. He cradles me against his hard chest, soft murmurs of words I don't understand. I suck in a deep breath, knowing it's Jim and not Mike. The anger that flowed through my veins is gone now, and all that's left in its wake is a sorrow I don't understand. Jim isn't Mike and I know that, but the fear still lingers.

A subtle tingle starts in my toes and works its way up through my legs to my torso and finally my arms. As it travels, it feels less like a tingle and more like a buzzing, but then a heaviness takes over me and it feels so right and perfect that I welcome it. Mike's image slowly fades from my mind, but before it disappears completely, I relive the worst moment of my entire life as Mike's blade pierces Ian's flesh. Blood spills from his small, frightened face, mixing with tears that stream his cheeks. Not my boy. Not Ian.

"No, Mike. No," I whisper to myself, knowing Jim can hear me and he's going to ask questions. I just can't stop myself. This moment still haunts me, despite the passage of time, it doesn't cease to hurt.

"Who the fuck is Mike and what did he do to you?"

When the fog lifts and it's just me and Jim once again, I stiffen in his arms. He's asking questions and demanding answers. Answers I don't want to give, moments I don't want to relive. But I have to. Because Jim doesn't want me and the only way to convince him of that is to tell him the truth about the woman he calls his girl.

"Won't ask again, babe."

"No," I say firmly. Once I tell him, this is all over, and he doesn't get to dictate my pain. "I'll tell you when I'm ready and I'm not ready now. You don't have to like it, but you do have to deal with it."

"Just tell me," he says softly and it breaks down my walls just a bit. "I want to know you. Every broken little part of you."

"Why?" I can't think of a single reason.

"I can't put you back together if I don't know where you're broken."

Sucking in a deep breath, I force myself to speak the words I never have before. Not to anyone.

CHAPTER ELEVEN

Mike Mancuso
Brooklyn, New York
November 12, 1994

There are some things no mother should ever have to experience, and the loss of her child is right there at the fucking top. If I'm not careful, my self-loathing is going to shine through my carefully crafted demeanor. *There's still time to back out*, I tell myself. But one look to my right, at my wife, and I know that the only way out of this situation is with a bullet between my ears.

"Roll up the window, Carlo," Esmeralda says.

Her voice is tinged with an irritation I almost never hear. I give it a minute before complying, letting the drops of rain hit my forehead and cheeks, bathing me in a kind of clarity I'm sorely lacking. My wife—my dear, sweet, quiet Esmeralda—refuses to use my preferred name. "Mike" isn't a boss's name, in her opinion. "Carlo" commands respect, and I'm the son of the boss, so I better be fucking respected. Not that it matters. If my men knew what I'm about to do, they wouldn't respect me. They might fear me as their *capo*, and they might do as they're told, but that's not respect. Fear doesn't buy loyalty—only respect does that.

Esmeralda clears her throat, and because I can't handle a disagreement about getting rain on the fucking leather of a car she didn't work to buy and doesn't even drive, I press the button, effectively cutting myself off from the outside world. A world where most people make it through their entire lives without getting blood on their hands. Inside this car, though, the world is a very different place. It's no place for children.

"What are you thinking?" Her voice is back to being soft and careful, as if I'm going to punish her for speaking.

"We could turn around," I say. My voice is even

and cool, as if I don't care. It's a lie. I care too much.

"Nonsense, honey. We're going to pick up our babies. You still want them, don't you?"

A disgusted laugh escapes me at the sound of the bullshit flying out of her mouth right now.

"It doesn't matter what I want."

"That's not true. We made a deal. I get Michael and Alexandra for my own in exchange for my acceptance."

Sliding over the seat, I sidle up to the woman I swore to love, honor, and protect, but I feel like doing none of that shit right now. "Acceptance?"

"I accept that, no matter how much I love you, we both know you married the wrong sister."

I turn my body toward her and drag my hand up the tops of her thighs, over her flat, barren stomach, between her breasts, and to her neck. My hand clamps down and squeezes until she gasps for air. My nose skims across her cheek, and I position my mouth near her ear.

"I do this for you, and you learn to keep your mouth shut. You are my wife, my property, not my fucking equal. This is my penance for liking the feel of your sister's pussy more than yours, but don't mistake this gift for anything more than it is. If I had my way, we'd forget your bitch sister exists."

I push her away and ignore her panicked gasping for breath as I slide back to my original position and roll my window down again.

"We are forgetting her. After this, she's gone," she says softly, almost fearfully. "It'll just be you and me and our babies."

"If you want those little complications to see their first birthday, I suggest you don't leave them alone with me. Accidents happen, especially at their age. I'd hate for your niece and nephew to drown during bath time."

"My son and daughter, Carlo," she snaps loudly and with an anger she's never exhibited before. "Those babies belong to me, not that bitch. You demand my submission, but you don't have the courtesy to respect what you're given. You want me to learn my role, well, daddy, you need to learn yours."

The driver pulls us up to the curb of a cheap motel and stops the car. I feel vaguely ill at what I just said but push it down. There's no room for weakness in my world, especially now. So I get out of the car, ignoring Esmeralda as she climbs out the other side.

We didn't always used to be like this. I met Ruby first, and then I met my wife. One pursued me, and the other had to be chased. Twins, but so very different. Nearly identical in everything but their coloring and demeanor, Ruby is pure fire and Esmeralda is icy cool. Ruby is loud and insufferably opinionated, while Esmeralda is what my father calls "the perfect Mafioso wife." The woman I married was perfect. At first. Once I'd resigned myself to taking Esmeralda as my wife, I reveled in her quiet power. The gentle way she would ask for things, the manner in which she supported my choices while still giving her opinion. She never once argued with me or fought for something if I'd already said no. Not until she found out about Michael and Alexandra, at least. I should have been pleased that she finally found something to fight for, but not this. This, she should have let go. But she didn't, and here we are.

I right my shoulders, straighten my back, and button the jacket of my suit. The motel before me is run down with chipping paint and crumbling plaster. Ruby didn't have to live like this. She had plenty of choices, but she didn't take any of them. I wish she'd just done as she was told to begin with. We could've had our family without me losing my marriage.

"She brought this on herself," I mutter to myself. Not quietly enough, though, and Esmeralda's jaw ticks when she hears it, but she says nothing. I take a look at my wife, the last look of her that I afford myself before I ascend the concrete steps up to Room 201 and become the man my father already thinks I am.

When I'm in front of the door, I stand and wait for my man, Benny, to come up with the key. The motel clerk wasn't hard to shake down. A couple rocks and he was giving her up. Personally, I hate drugs—they turn loyal men into rats—but that's the way the market's going, so the Mancuso organization has to evolve, or we'll get left behind.

Benny makes his way up the stairs. Stomping. He's slamming his feet down on the cement like we got nothing to lose here. This shit gets out of hand, and Benny—as much as I like the guy—might end up in a place his mother will never find him. As much as I'd hate to do it, I'd have to. My father would insist upon it. My wife would drive me crazy until I fixed it. Hell, even my mother would nag me to fucking death until I handled my shit. But Benny isn't thinking about the position he's putting me in. I don't say anything, though. He makes enough noise, pisses Ruby off, and maybe she'll shoot him for me. Only problem is I'd have to shoot her, then, and I'd prefer not to have to do that. What we're doing here is already bad enough.

I'm on autopilot as Benny starts talking to me about how we're going to play this out. We got my driver down by the street, keeping an eye out for trouble. We got one of Benny's soldiers in the office with the day clerk. Ruby has nowhere to run, is likely unarmed, and has three kids with her. She's not as much of a threat as Benny seems to think she is, but I let him keep yapping until he's satisfied we've handled all our shit. I sense Esmeralda about to open her mouth a few times, but a slight shake of my head ensures her silence.

"Open the door, Benedict." I wave an arm at the closed door. Benny takes his time inserting the key and turning the lock. My eyes fall closed, and I give myself this moment. I don't think about the first time I met Ruby or the way she looked at me. I don't indulge in all the memories I shouldn't hold close but do anyway. Instead, I focus on the last time I saw her and the hate that filled her eyes and her words. She promised to destroy me if I took the twins. She said she would kill me with her bare hands. I'm not supposed to show weakness, I'm not supposed to be afraid, but I was then and I am now. Ruby is tough. She knows how to survive.

I open my eyes and give my wife a look. She is stone-faced, callous even. I don't know how twin sisters could end up being so different, but I don't dwell on it. I let my hate for the woman at my side settle and burn in my chest. I let it consume me until all I can think of is making my life bearable once again. I loathe the man I see in the mirror, but I hate the woman in my bed even more. There is no divorce, no getting out. There is only one way to make this end, and that's by doing exactly what my family expects of me—by getting rid of the woman I love.

I kick open the door so hard that it bounces off the wall behind it. The room is small, with a variety of cheap pieces of luggage strewn about atop the old, worn furniture. A secondhand stroller sits between the bed and the wall. It's clean but a total piece of shit. I hate the idea of my children riding in that thing. On the other side of the bed is a sizable pile of plastic bags filled with a bunch of baby shit. Judging by Esmeralda's recent shopping trips, babies are expensive and need a lot of things. I wouldn't be surprised if the money I gave Ruby is almost out by now. She won't be able to support three kids for much longer anyway.

"Ruby," I shout. "I know you're here."

Esmeralda takes a step forward, but I put up an arm to block her movements. Benny keeps guard at the door, knowing better than to move. Having both my wife and my soldier in place, I move deeper into the room. I should draw my gun, but I don't. Maybe if Ruby shoots me, she'll put me out of my misery.

At the back of the room is a bathroom sink and mirror affixed to the wall. To left is a small closet that blocks the rest of the bathroom from view. It's a typical motel room setup, which is good, because there's only one place she could be hiding.

"We could make this easy, Ruby," I say with ease, taking a few more steps toward the bathroom. Still, she says nothing. Just when I'm doubtful that she really is here, I remind myself of the stroller. The twins are only a few weeks old. She can't get around without the stroller, especially with her son Ian in tow.

"Come out, Ruby. I won't hurt you."

A few more steps toward the bathroom and I stop. I crane my neck and open my ears as much as I can. Soft whispers are coming from the bathroom, followed by the choked sobs of a child. I walk as delicately as I can around the closet and focus in on the closed bathroom door. I can hear him much better from here. Ian is whispering to his mom, telling her everything is okay and he'll protect her. My stomach sinks.

I have to do this.

"Ian, dude. It's Uncle Mike," I say in my best kind voice. He's a little boy and he trusts me. I've known him since he was just a toddler, and we've always gotten along. Hell, I even like the kid.

"Mommy, it's okay. It's Uncle Mike." His little boy exuberance is almost too much to take. Despite his excitement and relief, Ruby lets out a frustrated sob.

"No, baby, no," she says.

"I'm here, buddy. Let me in."

"We're safe. Uncle Mike will make it better," Ian says. His little feet thump against the wall while he goes about talking to his mom. Soft baby whimpers quickly turn to loud screams. One baby at first and then two. They're in there. Right on the other side of the closed door. I just need Ian to open it for me.

Even if Ruby does have a weapon, she won't use it with Ian in the way.

The knob turns, and then the door opens slowly. Ian's small, pale face peeks out from the crack. There's a hopeful smile at play. When I smile back, he throws the door open and rushes toward me. I welcome him into a hug, lifting him up and holding his small body against mine.

The door creeps open. And there they are. My family. Ruby's wide brown eyes stare up at me from beneath a thick head of reddish-brown hair. Her cheeks are red and splotchy with fallen tears. She visibly swallows and clenches her jaw. Her body tenses as the cries from our children deepen and grow more concerning. Esmeralda's read up on babies in preparation for this day. She says a mother knows her baby's cries. Does Ruby know why they're crying?

"Please." Ruby's voice is shaky, breaking at the end. "Don't do this."

"I have to," I say. My voice is quiet, weak even. It's the one thing I can't afford—weakness. "Just put them down, okay? Get out of the tub and put them down."

"I can't," she says. The babies scream in her arms as she bounces them to try to calm them down. It doesn't work. I can't see their faces or who's who. Each of the twins are bundled in bright yellow blankets. But there they are. My children. My legacy. Father will be proud.

"You have to."

"No," she cries. Her eyes bounce between me and Ian, whose body tenses as he picks up on the fact that this isn't a friendly visit.

"These are my babies. You can't just take them from me."

"I don't have a choice." My body tenses as the sounds of Esmeralda's heels click on the floor behind me. The sound grows louder until she's directly behind me. Ruby's eyes widen, her jaw is slack, and her already wan complexion pales even further. She never has seen Esmeralda the way I see her. Cold, ruthless, unforgiving. After this, I can't imagine Ruby won't be able to see Esmeralda for who she really is. But it wouldn't be the first time she surprised me.

"Do it," my wife hisses in my ear. It's so quiet that I almost miss it.

Taking a deep breath, I pull out the knife—a

classic bayonet style from World War II—that once belonged to Ruby and Esmeralda's grandfather, and I place it against Ian's throat. He thrashes and pulls against me even as I tell him that he's going to hurt himself. The knife grazes his neck just enough to make him shout out in pain. I don't want to kill him. I can't kill him.

"Don't hurt my boy," Ruby warns. "You hurt my boy and you'll live to regret it."

"Get out of the tub and leave the children there." Jesus fucking Christ, if she would just get out of the fucking tub we could be done with this already.

"I'll have to hurt him if you don't get out of the tub."

Neither of us move or speak for a long time. Not even Esmeralda pipes up. Thank fuck. I can't stand here and beg the woman I... Ruby while my wife complains behind me. This is hard enough. My stomach tenses, my throat tightens, and if I'd been able to keep anything down this morning, I'd be convinced that I was about to throw it up right now.

"Essie, please," Ruby whispers, finally breaking the silence among the adults. Her eyes are fixed on her twin. Ian is still whimpering, but he's stopped moving. The babies cry and cry, waiting for their mother to attend to them.

"I can't. I'm sorry." Esmeralda's face is fucking priceless. Wide, tear-filled eyes, a trembling lower lip, and a scrunched brow. Everything about this woman makes me feel sick. I'm a monster, but at least I don't paint myself the victim. I am the vile things that are said about me. I am the son of Carlo Mancuso, Sr. I am the piece of shit that feels nothing for his wife but everything for her sister. I am all of that, and I fucking own it.

The severity of the moment gets to me. It's too much. Everybody wants something, and nobody here gives a fuck about what I want. My father didn't care what I wanted, so he tried to make me into the perfect *principe*. My wife didn't ask what I wanted, so she demanded a family. My mother didn't ask what I wanted, so she's getting Ruby out of the picture. One day, a long time ago, just before I lost my soul to the gold band on the fourth finger of my left hand, Ruby asked me what I wanted. Her. I wanted her. And I had her, but only briefly, and that's how we ended up here. It's all bullshit. The *Omerta*, the family, the code. This thing of ours. What a fucking joke.

Enough.

This has to end.

I'm not even thinking anymore. I'm just bringing the knife to the corner of Ian's eye, and I'm digging into his skin. He's crying, Ruby's crying, the babies are still crying. Esmeralda is silent. Her nephew is being sliced fucking open, and she's silent. I dig in deeper, my rage boiling over, enjoying the way the blood drips from his small, innocent face. If I don't stop, I'll slice into his eye and he'll go blind.

"Out of the tub," I demand. Ruby's moving now, quicker than I expect. She's trying to set them down, but she can't. I'm not sure how she managed it before—with Ian's help maybe. "Faster," I bark at her. I can't hold on to this for much longer. I can't continue to cut him open like he's a fucking fish. He's a child. Her child. And he's crying and thrashing about. He's got to be in some serious pain. There's more blood now, and it's coating the handle of the knife, making it slick.

Carefully, Esmeralda slips past me and Ian. She walks slowly, as if she's tiptoeing, toward the tub. I can't even hear the fake-ass bullshit she's saying to her sister on her approach. I catch a few words here and there. It's my fault. This is my idea. She's being forced into it. I could argue, but why should I? So Ruby can know the truth? I can't take that from her.

Right now, I'm taking everything else. I won't take the love she has for her bitch sister, too.

As Esmeralda convinces Ruby to put the babies down, I pull the knife back from Ian's eye. My hand shakes, my fingers slip on the handle, and I suck in a shaky breath. I'm not paying attention. The blade is still dug into his flesh, and I've created a scar halfway to his ear now. Esmeralda gets Ruby out of the tub, and she stands in front of her.

The moment my wife gives Ruby her back, Ruby's expression changes. She's less pained now, less fearful, but still angry and afraid, though. Not a foot in front of the tub, in the small bathroom, in the dingy motel, Ruby focuses her fierce brown eyes on mine. Reaching up, she grabs Esmeralda by the neck, produces a .22 from the back of her jeans, and pushes the barrel into the side of my wife's head.

"Put my son down or she's dead."

"You won't kill her," I say. My blades dances along Ian's skin from his ear to his mouth. The cut isn't nearly as deep as the first one, but it, too, will scar.

"Put him down!" Ruby's scream is that of a murderous lioness whose found her next meal. If I actually cared about my wife, I would be afraid. Ruby may not be the same kind of monster I am, but she's wild and unbroken. Until now. This is breaking her. Ruby could take a life—I just don't think she can take her sister's. Not even if she knew the real reason we're here.

"Kill her." A slow, callous smile creeps to my lips. The slack-jawed horror that finds its way to Ruby's face is priceless. She can't believe what I'm saying, but that's because she doesn't know her twin the way I do. She has no clue what lurks beneath the surface. I'm a monster, but her sister is a fucking beast.

"I'll keep them safe," Esmeralda says in that soft voice of hers. That soft, manipulative voice that makes you believe she is only ever gentle and passive. "I'll keep their names—Michael and Alexandra—I'll make sure they have the best life possible. Please. If you kill me, Carlo will kill you, and your babies won't have even a piece of either of us."

Ruby flinches. Her grip on the gun wavers, and even though I could live in utter fucking peace as a widower, I would have to kill Ruby, and I really don't want to have to do that. My father would demand to see the body. So, in an effort to speed things up, I wrap my hand around Ian's neck and start to squeeze. His cries are intense, and so is the jerking of his body.

"You can't have both, *tesoro*. It's Ian or the twins."

Ruby looks back at the babies in the tub, still wailing, and sobs a goodbye. She unloads the ammo from her .22 and drops it on the floor. Everything is so anticlimactic. Her movements are robotic, her expression dead. I want to say I almost feel bad for her, but I don't. I feel fucking awful, like a damn truck has run me over and then backed up just got good measure. She's no longer wild, no longer broken. This is devastation in a way I've never seen it before. When she's unarmed, she raises her hands in the air and focuses on Ian, telling him it's going to be okay. I back out of the room first and then direct her out of the bathroom and onto the bed. I'm still clutching the small, bloody boy. His cries are weakening, and the tension in his body is going slack. I've never hurt a kid before. We're not supposed to. I think he might be in shock, but what the fuck do I know?

After a minute, Esmeralda comes out of the bathroom, holding both babies in her arms. The smile on her face is undeniable even though she's trying to hide it. She has what she wants now, so maybe she'll be more tolerable. Probably not, but even condemned men can have some hope. My bitch wife takes the children to where Benny stands at the open door and whispers something in his ear before stepping around him and exiting the room completely. She disappears with a few clicks of her heels on the concrete.

I don't wait even a moment to let Ian go. He stumbles forward but loses his balance. With my open palm to the top of his back, I help him in his mother's direction with a slight shove. Ruby leaps forward and catches her boy. She grips his loose body with a ferocity I don't understand. She's a mother in a way I'm not a father. She's got years under her belt. I've barely gotten a good look at the twins in weeks. They probably look different than they did at the hospital. I don't fucking know. Not that looking at their faces would trigger some kind of parental instinct in me or something. Maybe they'll grow on me. If I'm lucky, our daughter will grow up to look nothing like her mother. Then, maybe, I'll be able to forget her fucking face.

"Hey, Benny," I call out, not moving from my spot.

He turns around. His eyebrows are raised, and he stares at me casually, like there's not a small child bleeding all over the place and a woman in hysterics.

That's Benny for you. He's a good guy. He's the best of this thing we got. Never lets me down.

"Yeah, Boss," he says with a head nod in my direction.

"What'd my wife tell you on her way out?"

He shrugs his shoulders—his tell—and shakes his head. "Nothing," he says. "She let me know she was heading to the car."

Benny's the best of us. His only flaw is the weak spot he has for my wife. Lord only knows the lengths he'll go for her. And I can't have somebody more loyal to her than to me.

"Cover his ears." My eyes are fixed on Ruby as she follows my instructions and cradles her boy in her lap, covering his ears and face as best she can.

Benny blinks, and it's only half a second later that his face shows the alarm I've been waiting for.

But it's too late.

I have my Desert Eagle raised and pointing at his face before he fully realizes what's happening. The bullet tears through the left side of his chest. He's on his back now, bleeding out all over the cheap motel carpet. Maybe now they'll replace the filthy shit. I step over what used to be Benny and avoid stepping in the blood as best I can. Esmeralda will fucking kill me if I track blood into the car. When I get to Ruby, she's got her chin raised and her eyes narrowed. Cold, angry, mean, she stares up at me. I tuck my gun away and fish a thick white envelope out of my suit jacket and throw it down next to her. She doesn't even follow the envelope. Her anger is palpable. If looks could kill...

"A paramedic's going to be by in a few minutes. He'll patch up the kid. You got enough money there to start over elsewhere." I suck in a deep breath and bend, bringing my face to her level before grabbing the back of her neck. "Now, do what you were fucking told and disappear."

I take in her scent one last time and place my lips to her forehead. It's fucked, I know, but I can't help myself. She's stock still. Even when I release her and walk away, she doesn't move. And I don't look back, because I can't bear to see the hatred in her eyes one more time.

CHAPTER TWELVE

Jim
Fort Bragg, California
July 23, 1997

The school secretary hands over the visitor pass with a warm smile on her face. She makes it a point to say that the school doesn't normally do this, that she's giving me something because—in her words—Ian's such a great kid. Damn straight, lady. My woman's raised a fucking awesome kid, and she's doing a damn good job of giving Ryan the mom he never had.

"You have fun today, Mr. Stone."

"Thanks." I step back and then pause. I've always been a shit parent. I don't even lie to myself about it. My boy would rather stay with a woman he only met a few months ago, and I let him because he deserves her. She's better than me, so much fucking better, and this proves it. Ruby knows their teacher's name. She knows which classroom they're in. She knows everything about those two kids. I'm an idiot.

"Is there something wrong, Mr. Stone?"

"I don't know where I'm going."

"That's okay," she says in a really encouraging voice. I hate that voice. It's the sound of judgment. Like she wants me to feel better about being a fuckup.

"The boys are in Mrs. Rhodes's class." She smiles. I stare at her blankly. She looks around awkwardly before she realizes that means nothing to me and directs me toward their classroom. I've only been to this school a handful of times and, even then, only ever to the office. My boy gets in trouble a lot—or he did. I don't know. I'd have to ask Ruby if he's still getting in trouble. Not that I'm going to ask her that after the shit she laid on me.

It's been a couple weeks since we talked about it.

I knew my woman had damage, but the Italian fucking mafia. Jesus Christ. I let that sink in one more time as I walk down the covered hallways of the elementary school, careful to remember the secretary's directions. Down the main corridor, to the second building on the left, third classroom. Clouds move overhead, casting a shadow across the sun's rays. Fuck. Not today. I can't have this shit today. First it'll be overcast, then the sky will break, and finally it'll be pouring goddamn rain and everything I've done will be for nothing.

Standing in front of the classroom door with the stupid permission slip in my hand, I suck in a deep breath. All the windows on this side of the building are high up, near the ceiling, save for a small square window at eye level, in the center of the bright blue door. I peer in and freeze.

There must be about ten students in the room, a much smaller number than during the school year. There are two little girls huddled together at one long table, their refuge among the sea of boys surrounding them. But that's not what has my blood running cold—it's the sight of the skinny, pale-faced boy with wavy light brown hair and large, sad brown eyes. He sits hunched over in his chair, his hands in his lap, and his bottom lip pulled between his teeth. Ryan sits beside him, a scowl on his face, his eyes focused up on the ceiling. A woman in her thirties, who I assume is their teacher, stands in front of Ryan with her hands on her hips. She's pissed about something, and knowing my boy, there's no telling=. That doesn't bug me. The kid isn't bothered by her, so neither am I. It's Ian that makes me take pause. I squint my eyes and stare at the red, angry scar that mars his face. He's been scratching at it, I can tell. It's not normally this red or obvious. Their teacher keeps going. Ryan rolls his eyes. And while the two of them are in some kind of battle of wills, Ian continues to sink further and further into himself. His hand comes up to his face and scratches at his scar. He flinches on contact and rocks himself back and forth. His movements are small, inconspicuous. Nobody seems to notice. Except I do. I see this boy with all his pain and damage. I see his heart and his mother's spirit that lives in him so brightly. I see this kid who's been through some serious shit and the way he just caves in on himself. It's not fucking right, and I'm going to make this better for him. I have to.

Turning the knob and pushing the door open, I try to avoid the curious looks from all the kids but mine.

The lady, Mrs. Rhodes, turns my way and

blanches. She forces a smile to her face and, with tight lips, says, "Can I help you?"

"Yeah, I'm here for my boys," I say and bridge the gap between us. Reluctantly, I hand over the fucking permission slip. It's ridiculous that I have to explain myself. These are my kids. Well, the smug-looking one making rude faces at his teacher's back is definitely mine. The other one is mine, too. His momma just doesn't know it yet.

"Okay, well, we're in the middle of an assignment right now." She turns her head toward the boys, catching Ryan's expression. She clenches her jaw and tries to calm herself down. My mouth twitches as I fight to keep the smile off my face. He's such a little asshole, and I'm a shit parent for enjoying this. If Ruby were here, she'd shut him down real quick, but that's what mothers are for.

From beside Ryan, Ian sits up a little straighter now. His face is a mix of worry and fear—and more of the latter than the former. His eyes volley between his teacher and Ryan with an alarm that worries me. I could tell this Rhodes lady that he's freaking out and I need to get him home, but I'm not going to do him like that. He's nine today—fucking nine—and it's time he and Ryan start learning how to be a men. I can't teach them how to handle their own shit if I run to his rescue.

"How about you just send it home with them. We got shit to do, and their mom's waiting on us."

"Language, Mr. Stone." Mrs. Rhodes's jaw ticks in irritation. "Their mom? I thought. .." she trails off.

"Boys, pack up. We're going," I say without taking my eyes off of the woman in front of me. I don't bother explaining the situation to her. She wouldn't get it anyway.

We make it out of the classroom and to the van before either of them speaks.

"That was so cool, Dad!" Ryan shouts from the backseat. He bounces in place. Leave it to my kid to be fucking excited over me telling his teacher off. While Ryan chatters about whatever the fuck it is that his teacher did to piss him off this time, Ian sits in his seat in silence with his brows pulled together.

"Hey, bud. What's going on over there?" I keep one eye on the road and the other on the quiet boy behind me. He doesn't respond, so I try again. "Why are you so quiet?"

"Where's my mom?"

"She's at the clubhouse." He's opening up, which

is good. It also gives me something to focus on aside from the fact that I'm driving a fucking minivan. I bought the stupid thing as kind of a joke for the little woman, but since this was the only thing available for me to pick the boys up in, it's not fucking funny anymore. I'm trading this goddamn thing in for something I can be seen in around town. If any of my brothers see me in this mom-mobile, they might take my fucking cut.

After a quick stop by the trailer park in town to pick up Josh—the boys' friend who somehow managed to evade summer school—the four of us head toward the park. Might be the first time in my life, but we're running early, and I have to circle the lot a few times before I give up and put the car in park. Keeping three rowdy boys contained in one vehicle without issue takes some kind of special mastery I don't have. By the second lap around the park, all three are unbuckled and Ryan and Josh are wrestling. They probably shouldn't be doing that, but fuck it. They bump their damn heads, they might learn to sit the fuck down. Christ, I don't know how Ruby does it all day.

"Ow!" Ryan screams from the very back of the van. One of his legs is stuck straight up in the air as it kicks relentlessly at Josh's side as he keeps my boy pinned down. The kid deserves it, so unless there's blood, I'm staying in my fucking bubble. Ian's in the seat in front of them, facing the back, and he's actively coaching Ryan in how to get out of Josh's hold. The kid has a surprising amount of knowledge regarding wrestling maneuvers.

"Dad, help!" Ryan screams. I smile to myself and turn around in my seat to get a better view.

"Just tap out. He's got you pinned," Ian says with a sigh. Already bored of the action, he turns around and faces me. "Are you going to help him?"

"Do you think I should?"

Ian thinks on it for a moment before he grins and shakes his head. "No," he says. "He started it."

"You know if you need it, I got your back right?" He nods his head and gives me an unenthusiastic, "Yeah", but I can tell he doesn't mean it. The boy's probably had a lot of men promise him shit they couldn't deliver throughout his life. "I'm gonna show you. Every single day, I'm gonna be here for you. You and your mom."

He doesn't say anything. He just stands there, watching me for a long moment before his eyes get really big and the largest grin I've ever seen spreads across his face. His eyes are firmly focused on something behind me.

Ruby.

When I turn around, I see her. She's standing in front of the minivan, hands on her hips and a smirk on her face. She raises an eyebrow at me and shakes her head. Ian and I fight to see who can get out of the mom mobile first. I think he wins by a hair, but I'm so focused on my own pursuit that I don't push it when the kid jumps out of the side door and screams, "I win!"

"We weren't even racing!" I shout and scoop him up in my arms. My back aches as I spin him around in circles. He's not nearly as small as he was even a few months ago. "You're a cheat!"

Ian squeals in delight and reaches out for Ruby, just barely missing her outstretched arms as we make another circle. He's laughing a full belly laugh that warms my fucking heart. He could probably do this forever, but my head is already spinning, so I set him down and gather my bearings.

"Doesn't matter. Momma cheats all the time and gets away with it."

"Does she now?" My question is for Ian, but my eyes are for Ruby. She's smiling at us in a way that makes it impossible for me to not smile back. It's not the happy, joyful smile I give our boys. It's different. I don't know how exactly. I just know it doesn't feel quite the same.

"She cheated during Monopoly last week," Ryan says, bouncing toward us. Josh follows, rubbing one eyes and using the other to glare at my kid. As Josh passes, his eyes meet mine and I pat him on the back. Josh is a little taller than Ryan, but my kid's a fucking bruiser.

"I did not!" Ruby's eyes are wide as she stares down at Ryan in fake disbelief.

"Yes you did. You also said liars get their butt spanked!" Ryan darts around me with an outstretched open palm, but I catch him before he can smack her.

"Hey, that ass is mine," I say with narrowed eyes at my son. He glares back at me, and I swear to Christ the kid is my fucking clone. God help the entire goddamn world. When I fix my attention back on Ruby, I lick my lips and watch as her eyes heat. Jesus fuck, this woman could kill me with a single moan. She's going to moan for me one of these days, and my heart is just going to give out right then and there.

"Tell me there's a reason these punks aren't in school," she says. Her tone is a mix of hopeful and suspicious, but she's not pissed, so that's something.

"There is," I say and pull a red bandanna out of my back pocket and bend down to face Ian. He stares at me, almost nervously, but I smile, and he relaxes in response. "I'm gonna put this on your eyes. Is that okay with you?"

His eyes automatically dart to Ruby's, and after a thoughtful moment, he nods his head. Trust is everything with this kid. With Ryan, you can just grab him and blindfold his ass. He'll pitch a fit about it, but he won't be distressed. Knowing everything Ian's been through, much less with a man he trusted and looked up to, I can't do the same with him. He needs to trust me so I can help him work through his shit. So when I reach up and put the blindfold around his eyes, I'm talking to him the whole time. Mostly, I'm telling him about Ryan's last birthday when he got us kicked out of the pizza place. That ban lasted for almost an entire month before the owner realized how much pizza the club orders and lifted it for the sake of his business. Still, I can't say it wasn't embarrassing to have my kid break into that machine that's totally rigged but is supposed to give you a chance to grab and win a stuffed animal. Even after I told him to give back the quarters he'd gotten out, he still managed to make it home with almost four bucks in his shoes. I was pretty proud of the little asshole, if I'm being honest.

"What are we doing?" Ruby's biting her lip. She watches me as I stand up and place a hand on Ian's back.

"We're throwing a fucking party here," I say. "It's Ian's birthday, isn't it?"

Her eyes widen to the size of saucers before the tears start. The fucking tears. I pretend not to notice and just shrug off her reaction like it's not a big deal even though I know damn well it is a big deal for her and her son. I just don't like the tears. Thank fuck she has a son and not a daughter. I don't know how I'd handle all the crying.

My steps falter with the thought. She *does* have a daughter. She also has another son. They're not here, but that doesn't mean they don't exist or matter to her. Ian was old enough when they were born to remember them. I know Ruby talks about them as much as she can so that Ian never feels like they're forgotten or disposable. That's the worst thing, she said, the idea that Ian might think she could just toss a kid aside. She couldn't, but he's a little kid, and he needs to be reminded of that fact and often. I can't give her back the time she's lost, but I'm going to try like hell to make sure she's reunited with them one day. I haven't asked her anything else about the twins since she told me about them. I don't know what to say. Every time I think about that motherfucker who hurt her, I want to kill someone. She begged me to leave it alone, so I have. For now. But the first chance I get, those babies are coming home, and fuck anybody who gets in my way.

"What did you do?" Her voice is a mix of amazement and curiosity.

"Something you were afraid to do," I say and don't meet her eyes. I know why she didn't plan a party for him. She doesn't want to give him something he might not ever get again. But what she doesn't know is that this isn't a one-time deal. This is the first of many we're going to have as a family, and even though she's not ready to admit that yet, I am. Ruby gets my boy in a way no woman ever has. She tolerates me and my shit like nobody else ever could. So fuck her doubts. She's ours.

Looking at my woman, I see the tears clearing from her eyes. I kind of like it, knowing they're happy tears. Feeling a little fucking romantic, I take her hand in mine and give it a squeeze. We walk across the park and over the hill that separates the lot I parked in from the playground where my mom has the party set up. When we get to the top, we stop and I grin to myself at the gasp that escapes my girl.

The trees surrounding the playground have been decorated with balloons. Ma's already got three of the grill stations going with burgers and hot dogs, and the entire club is here. Grady's got his woman here, and she's starting to show, so I know we're going to have a new little fuck running around soon. Chief's daughter, Elle, is on the swings, trying to see who can pump higher with Butch's daughter, Nicole. Across from the crowd of adults is Butch's woman, Sheryl, and their baby, Jeremy. Kid was just barely hatched and he's already got a handful of lost girls losing their shit over him.

"You didn't." Ruby's got her free hand over her mouth, and the fucking tears are back, but I don't care. She's happy, and fuck if that doesn't make my entire goddamn day. It makes riding around in that minivan like a bitch totally worth it.

"You ready, Ian?"

"Yeah," he says with a shout. I remove the

blindfold from his eyes and pat him on the back.

"Happy birthday, son."

"No shit?" Ryan's curse earns a slap on the back of his head from Ruby. I have to fight off a laugh.

"No shit," I say and give Ryan and Ian a push toward the playground. "Go. Have fun!"

They don't wait for further instruction. The three boys dart off toward the playground. Ian goes for the slide while Ryan heads to the monkey bars. Josh, as predicted, slides up beside my mom and starts sniffing the air while eyeing the food. The kid won't stop growing, so it's no wonder he's hungry all the time.

"You did this," Ruby whispers. She moves to stand in front of me and stands on her tiptoes to place a kiss on my cheek. It's not exactly the kind of kiss I prefer, but I'll take it.

"Little boys deserve big parties."

She nods her head and blinks away the tears that are threatening to fall. In an attempt to stop that shit before it gets out of hand, I pull her against me and walk us to the playground. She's reluctant at first, her eyes still wet, but eventually catches on and pulls it together.

We're barely at the decorated trees before Sheryl meets us with baby Jeremy in her arms. She grins at my woman and bounces on her feet. "Surprise!"

"You knew?" Ruby asks in shock.

Sheryl laughs a little too loud and scares the baby, but she bounces him in her arms to calm him down.

"Of course I knew," Sheryl says. "We *all* knew."

One look at Ruby and her eyes are watering again. Oh for fuck's sake. I gesture to Sheryl to hand the baby over, and when she does, I peer down at the kid and smile. His eye color isn't fully developed yet, but they're already a striking blue.

"Babe," I say and hand him to Ruby, "You want something to cry over. Hold this little asshole."

"God, he gets cuter every time I see him," she says.

As Sheryl and Ruby lose themselves in small talk about the baby that turns into shit talk about Layla using while pregnant, I silently make a break for it. Another minute talking about Layla and the women will be demanding I do something about it, and since I don't know what the fuck to do, or if there's anything I can do, I opt out of the situation entirely. Today's been a good day. I don't want to ruin it by thinking about things I can't change.

So instead of worrying about all the fucking bad that looms over us, I go meet my sons on the playground and see if I can fit my ass down that slide Ian's obsessed with.

CHAPTER THIRTEEN

Ruby

Jim's standing across the main room in the clubhouse. Maybe thirty feet at most, but it's too far. I just want him closer. After waking up today, convinced the entire day was going to suck, only for him to turn it around for me... I need him here. Like now.

"Seems my boy can do more than just fuck things up," Sylvia says from beside me. She purses her lips and then takes a long draw from her bottle of beer. My eyes linger on her pale features and thinning hairline for too long. She shrinks back from me and focuses on the wall behind the bar.

"I can't believe he did all that," I say. It's the truth. Even Mike didn't do shit like that for my boy. Sure, he'd bring him by a toy the week of his birthday, but beyond that, it was like the kid didn't exist. I'd just kind of accepted the fact that Ian's birthday would always be a kind of solemn day. We've always celebrated it, just the two of us, with a private little party at home. One year he got cookies, the next he got cupcakes. One year he got a single cupcake—it was all I could afford at the time—but he acted like that lone cupcake was made of gold with the way he thanked me for it. And that's not normal or right. Kids should take cupcakes for granted.

"Of course he did," Sylvia says. "Ian's his boy, too."

My eyes fall closed at her words. Ian isn't really Jim's. As much as I appreciate the club wanting him to feel like he's part of the family, I can't let this continue. Ian is *my* son. I carried him in my body and safely delivered him in a hospital in Tampa. I fought to get him to latch on, and I'm the one who diapered him. I taught him to read and write. I've fed and clothed him since the day he was born. I put that boy through hell and then pulled him back out of it. That's on me. I've been the only parent, only fucking constant in this kid's life since even before he was born. It might take a village to raise a kid, but history's shown me that people leave. My heart is going to break when Jim decides we're too much trouble, and that's fine, but I won't let my boy feel like he's lost one more thing. So no, fuck that. Ian is *mine*.

"I know that look," Sylvia says. Her tone is of defeat rather than irritation. I hear a lot of that from her these days. She always sounds so tired and fed up, not even frustrated, just doing her best to keep on living.

"My boy finally has something stable. I don't want to take that from him by letting Jim play daddy. When this ends, it's only going to hurt Ian."

"And if it ends, you won't be hurt?"

"That's not what I meant," I say.

"No, I don't suppose it is," she says. Finally, she turns in her seat to face me. I do the same and when I meet her eyes, I find an exhaustion there that surprises me. I see the woman almost every day. She's become a surrogate mother to me, treats Ian like he's her own. Sylvia Stone is family, and if we ever have to leave, it's going to break both our hearts.

"And what if it doesn't end?"

"That's the fairy tale, right? Nobody goes into anything wanting it to end, but shit happens. Jim thinks he can handle my baggage now, but it will get too much for him."

"The Mancuso thing?" She's smiling all coy and knowing, as if she didn't just drop a huge bomb on me. For the first time in months, she looks healthy. A confusing mix of gratitude and fear overtakes me. It's overwhelming.

"Didn't know you knew about that."

"They might not get along that well, but Jim is his father's son. His loyalty to Forsaken is unwavering."

"He told them," I whisper. There's a brief panic that spikes before it settles. I just sit there, soaking it in. The club knows. Jim fucking told his brothers about my history. It's no small detail for anyone to drop on the club, much less the VP.

"I don't know what to say."

"You want my opinion?"

"Not really," I admit.

Sylvia shakes her head in response, her smile growing with every passing moment. Her lips part and a laugh escapes. She's a good woman, and I think I forget how much I rely on her to keep me sane. I haven't had a mother in years, much less a good mother. I can't imagine living without her now that I have her.

"I think you need to trust in a man who puts his cut on the line for you."

"But I don't want him to put his cut on the line for me. That's not right."

"Sweetheart, it's the most right thing he's ever done," she says.

I give her a resigned smile and push away from the bar. Sylvia and I can talk more later, if we must. For now, there's something I need to do. And he's standing across the room with a beer in his hand and a large, totally chill smile on his face.

And I love him.

Holy hell, do I love him.

I don't even care if this turns around to bite me in the ass later. Right now, I just need him. I need to touch him and be held by him. The sun has already set, and the boys are passed out in the chapel, surrounded by a pile of empty Pixy Stix wrappers. I don't need to play mommy for the time being. Right now, I'm just Ruby. I'm a woman who's in love with a man and desperately needs to be with him.

Jim's focus is on a conversation he's having with Grady. They're talking business, so I don't interrupt. Instead, I just slide up beside my man and cozy into his side when he wraps an arm around my shoulders. The guys don't talk business out in the open if they want to keep it from us, but it's still not our place to chime in, so I don't. The conversation lasts a few more minutes, with Grady bringing up what I think are some solid points about switching up transport routes. Jim agrees on principle but is hesitant for the club to take any action now. It's a whole lot of mumbo jumbo that I try not to understand. The less I know about the details of their business, the happier I am. When Layla starts calling for Grady, the guys wrap it up and end with Jim agreeing to bring up Grady's ideas to Rage.

"What do you think?"

"He's a good guy," I say, figuring that's what Jim means. It's an odd question, but my head is buzzing with anticipation, and I'm not thinking clearly.

"Fuck that prick," Jim says with a grumble as he pulls me closer. "I meant about his ideas."

"I'm sure you'll take them to Rage and the two of you will weigh your options."

Diplomacy has never been my strong suit, but the longer I'm around Sylvia the better I'm getting. Jim asks what I think of the club's potential for changing up their transport options, and I know damn well that he's not asking me to give him my opinion. Those kinds of questions are for old ladies and not possible girlfriends, buddies, whatever the hell we are.

Jim gives me a hard look I don't expect. It's almost a warning, but for what I don't know. Bringing the beer bottle to his lips, he tilts his head back and takes a long pull, finishing it off, then leaves the bottle on a nearby table. Without another word, Jim removes his arm from around my shoulders, and before I can object to the loss of contact, he grabs my hand in his and pulls me to him.

"I asked for your opinion." His voice is stern but not angry.

"And I don't want to give it," I say. His eyes narrow incrementally in response, but I don't let it deter me. He might think he wants my opinion on club business, but I'm certain he'd much rather wait in favor of what I have in mind.

Stepping up on my tiptoes, I pull Jim closer to me and breathe him in. He smells of soap and cigarettes, a perfect combination. My lips press against his stubbled chin, and I soak in the lingering taste of chocolate and strawberries from Ian's cake. I didn't realize until today exactly how much Jim loves his sweets. It's the little things like this that remind me of who he is. Flawed, yes, but he's also a good man. A good man who tries his best even when his best isn't quite good enough. A man who throws a birthday party for a little boy he doesn't have to care for but does anyway. This is the man I've fallen in love with.

"What'cha doing, Momma?"

"Showing my appreciation." The words are whispered against his rough jawline. He stills a moment before moving in, and then his lips are on mine. I breathe him in, reveling in having him this close to me, touching me, kissing me. I suck in his bottom lip and relish in the moan he gives me. My arms are around his neck, legs around his waist, and I'm hanging on for dear life. We're a tangled mess of limbs and sounds that are better suited for a private space.

When Jim pulls away, he's breathing heavily, barely able to form the words as he says, "Fuck."

Before I know it, we're on the move toward the hallway. I bounce in his arms, holding so tight that I hope I leave a mark so that everybody knows who Jim was with tonight. I might not have him forever, but I can leave a lasting impression.

There are hoots and hollers from the people around us as Jim carries me down the hallway to his room. The closer we get to being alone, the more my hands shake. My belly does flips, and my entire body is buzzing with excitement. I want this. I want it so bad that I can practically taste my own desperation. When he kicks the door open, I practically jump. I want nothing more than to be with Jim, but I can't control my nerves.

"Don't," he says, setting me down on my feet and stepping away. He stands in the doorway, his arms hanging limply at his sides. He leans in, placing his hands on either side of the door frame, and practically snarls at me. I blink.

"Don't think you have to do this because of today," he says. I open my mouth to respond, but he doesn't let me. "Just don't."

"Why did you do that? Today? Why did you do that?" My voice is firm, demanding even. I just can't let something that started so good end so badly before it even begins.

"You're seriously asking me that fucking question?" Jim's jaw ticks as he spits the words out at me. He pushes off the door frame, leans down, and breathes heavily in my face. It's always like this with us—hot tempers, angry words, and unspoken confessions. But not tonight.

"Tell me why."

"I fuck up a lot, okay? I fuck up and do shit I can't make right. But this? I figured I could at least give Ian a fucking party."

"But why did you want to?" Gently, I place my hands on his chest and slide them underneath his cut. He huffs as I slide his cut off his shoulders and let it fall to the floor.

"Isn't it obvious?" he says. His hands toy at the hem of my shirt. With his eyes boring into mine, he stills. I nod, giving him the okay, and before I know it, my shirt is being pulled over my head.

We move quickly now, not waiting or thinking about what we're doing. He only stops long enough to kick the door shut behind us and make sure it's locked. I have my fingers pulling at the button of my jeans, but he stops me and finishes the job himself. His hands slip between the fabric of my pants and my skin, parting the two and sliding the jeans down over my hips. He sinks to his knees as he goes, never taking his eyes off mine.

I bend down so our faces are level, my lips trail kisses up from the base of Jim's throat to his chin and up to the corner of his eye. Jim isn't Mike, and he isn't Ian's dad. He's not any of the awful men who came before him. He gave me a job, a place my boy can settle in, and friends. Jesus, Jim's given us both so much. I can't repay him. No matter how hard I try, I won't ever be able to. So instead of trying, I let my touch tell him everything I can't.

"My kid's mom was some whore I'd see when the club would make it down to Oakland. She was pretty, but the kind of pretty that has to try too hard to be pretty." I don't know why he's telling me this, much less choosing now to say it. I like him sharing, though, so I just listen and watch as he strips me of my shoes and then my jeans and finally my socks. "There were girls in school I liked. Usually the mouthy ones who got in trouble. I can't remember any of their names."

Jim kisses his way up my foot to my leg and up to the inside of my knee. He lets his eyes fall, so focused on what he's doing, moving so slowly. Every single touch is like a lightning bolt to my heart.

Gripping me around the back of my thighs and pulling me closer, Jim's breath is hot against the fabric of my old, worn panties. They're not special or attractive. I didn't plan on this, or I would have put more thought into what I'm wearing.

"There were others." His breath is like a whisper to my core—a promise of what's to come. Gently, he places a kiss right there. It's just over the material, but the heat bypasses it and ghosts across my skin. With every word he speaks, my core heats and dampens even more. I didn't think I could want him more than I already did.

"I don't remember anything about the girls in school. I couldn't even remember Ryan's mom's name until the social worker showed up with him."

The conversation is decidedly not sexy, but the way his fingers grip the waistband of my panties, the way his hot breath warms my skin, and the roughness of his voice is the sexiest thing I've ever experienced.

Jim slips my panties down my legs, leaving me

exposed. I've never reveled in being so vulnerable to anyone before. But this is Jim, and I love him. I want to show him all of me—even the ugly parts.

"You were wearing tight jeans that hugged your ass perfectly and a black tank top that still gets me hard every time I see you wear it," he says. My head swims, but he doesn't explain. Instead, he grips my thighs again, holding them tight. He dips his face to the apex of my thighs, his nose skimming my soft curls.

I suck in a deep breath as his tongue jets out and slides along my folds. My head falls back, my eyes close, and I do my best to stay in the moment. Jim's tongue laps at my folds and skims through to my bud. I reach out and thread my fingers through his hair, holding it tight as he works me over. My arms and legs tingle, my core beats dramatically in rhythm to Jim's licks. His other hand reaches around and kneads my ass. A single finger traces the center line of my ass and dips between my cheeks. I don't want ass play, but I can't bring myself to say it. My lungs are already straining to suck in enough breath to keep me from passing out, but my fear turns out to be for nothing. His finger skims past my ass and beneath my cheek, then around my outer thigh and to my curls. His finger and tongue work together to create the most beautiful buzz that spreads throughout my entire body. His tongue and lips at my bud, sucking and lapping. His finger circles my pussy and then slowly slides inside. I gasp and try to catch my breath, but it's no use. Jim slides another finger into my wet pussy, teasing me relentlessly. In and out. Again and again. The throbbing builds, becoming more demanding, needing a release. My limbs burn hot, desperate to just let go already, but I can't. I want to, but it's not happening. Jim's ministrations falter just a moment before he changes positions and moans into my folds, creating a blissful sensation that quickly spreads to my legs and torso and even to the tips of my toes. Everything disappears for a moment as I lose myself to my release.

"Your hair was down. You were tired and nervous, but so fucking gorgeous," he says. I try to let his word sink in, but he's pulling me in his arms and carrying me to the bed. My legs are still shaking from the power of my orgasm, and my head is still swimming. I pry my eyes open in time to watch Jim as he sheds his clothes. For a man who drinks as much as he does, his body is incredible. All taut muscles, accented by tanned skin and tattoos. He has surprisingly muscular legs and a six pack I don't expect. Jim is, of course, stupidly handsome with a great body, but it's his eyes that have me biting my bottom lip in anticipation. Gray eyes that he gifted to his son stare down at me as he grabs a condom from the bedside table and then lowers himself to the bed. The tearing sound from the opened wrapper draws my attention to the apex of his thighs. I gulp at the sight of his hard dick. He's long and thick and pretty much everything a woman could ask for. It juts out from his body at the perfect angle. I don't even realize I'm rubbing my tender thighs together until Jim licks his lips and offers me a soft smile. It's almost shy even. Something that is so not the Jim I know and is endearing enough to somehow make me want him even more.

"You asked me why," Jim says. He rolls on the condom and parts my legs. He runs his hands over my thighs. His eyes darken as he guides himself to my entrance, but he pauses before even touching me. He has his free arm holding his torso off my body. The cords of his arm muscles are so close that I take the opportunity to place a kiss to them. His strong arms that lift our boys up, that keep him upright on his bike, and carry my groceries from the car to my kitchen are so important to who he is—to what he does—hold him above me. And I love these arms for what they do.

"Because I love Ian the same way I love Ryan.

Maybe that's fucked. I don't know, but I do. I love that kid, and I want to give him better. I want to give him a family."

I don't have time to absorb what he's just said because he's sliding into me, inch by glorious, tight inch. All I can think is that we're a perfect fit, he and I. And he wants to give my boy something he's never had before. Beyond a family, he wants to give him a dad. It's so big and epic that I might cry from the feeling of him filling me up both physically and emotionally.

Once he's buried himself inside me, he stills and looks directly into my eyes.

"I barely remember my son's mother. Spent almost a year hooking up with her. One look at you and every single detail is etched into my brain. That's why. Because even if you didn't want me, you're it for us."

He starts moving, slowly at first, before picking up the pace. He feels incredible inside me, even with the barrier between us. *Us.* He said, *You're it for us.* He's not just thinking of himself but of Ryan as well. Of course he thinks of Ryan, but the confirmation is enough to accelerate my heart rate. Noticing my reaction to what he's said, Jim slides a hand between us and finds my clit. He puts the faintest amount of pressure on my swollen nub and makes a circular motion. It's slow and glorious, but he's sure to pick up the speed little by little. My toes curl and legs spasm. I grab hold of his ass and squeeze, encouraging him to pick up the pace. What was once smooth, calculated movements becomes frantic and desperate with need. I'm making noises that should embarrass me, loudly and without apprehension. He's slamming into me with a force that might hurt if he wasn't hitting all the right spots. My nails dig into his flesh, leaving more marks, signs that we were together.

"That good for you, baby?" Jim's gasping for breath, his words broken.

Yes.

"I love you."

Once I've said the words, I want to take them back. More than anything, I'd like a do-over. Jim doesn't say anything. He just keeps going, but harder now, more furious. His free hand twists at my clit, sending me over the edge. I'm gasping for breath, desperate for the coming euphoria. My body is so tight I think I might snap in two, and then, just like that, the dizziness settles in and I'm floating on cloud nine. It's even better than the first one, because now Jim's following suit and falling apart above me. And when we're done, we lie like that, with him inside me, and no desire to clean up. I do my best to relax and enjoy the moment, but like an idiot, I told him I love him.

Just when I think he's fallen asleep, he slides out of me, kisses me, practically devouring my mouth, and then pushes off the bed. Pulling the condom off, he tosses it into the trash can near the bed and stands in the doorway to the en suite bathroom.

"Gotta shower and then get home, babe." With that, he disappears into the bathroom and turn on the shower. I wait for a moment, unsure of what to do. Moments drag into minutes, and my anxiety spikes. I don't know what Jim meant when he said I'm "it" for him and Ryan, but he sure as hell didn't return the sentiment when I told him I love him. He just continued to fuck me. He might like me, might like fucking me, and might sure as hell like how I take care of his boy, but he doesn't love me. And that's now painfully obvious.

So I run. Like an embarrassed fool, I run out of the room half-dressed and looking for my boy. I'm careful to be quiet as I scoop him up from the chair he's fallen asleep in in the chapel and even quieter as

I sneak us out of the clubhouse. Thankfully, it's a short walk to the apartment, because he's nine now and that means he's not really a little boy anymore.

Even though Jim says he wants to give Ian a family, he just broke me in the worst way. It should be a dull sort of agony, but it's not. It's a sharp pain that burns and grows from my heart out through the rest of me. This was a difficult but necessary reminder that I can't count on anyone else and I'm the only one Ian can rely on.

CHAPTER FOURTEEN

Somewhere in my subconscious, I recognize the sound of a lock clicking and the squeak of an opening door. I can't bring myself to move, though. I should, but I don't sense any danger—at least that's my excuse—so I try to drift back to sleep. It's Ian with the bathroom door, I'm sure. He's gotten better about waking up in the middle of the night if he has to pee. Moments later, hot breath ghosts against the back of my neck, which doesn't help me in the whole getting back to sleep thing. My kid has this thing about going pee and then being wide awake and chatty as fuck. It sucks, but it's just part of the glamorous life of a parent. I settle into the mattress, ignoring the way it dips behind me, and fight to keep my eyes closed. If Ian knows I'm awake, he's going to start talking to me.

As it is, he's probably staring at the back of my head right now, just hoping I'll give myself away. I love my boy, but holy crap do I not want to try to carry on a conversation first thing in the morning. It was hard enough to get him to sleep tonight. He couldn't stop talking about his birthday party and everybody who was there, but most of all, he wouldn't stop talking about Jim. He asked me twice if I thought Jim was nice and if I thought he would stay. Both questions broke me. I don't have an answer to either. Instead of lying to my boy, I just kept giving him candy and random snacks we have around the house. I didn't score any points for mom of the year today, that's for sure. The kid pokes me in my back, and when I don't respond, he does it again. And again. It's a good thing I love this kid, because he's one persistent little jerk sometimes.

"What time is it?" I mumble when I realize that the kid isn't going to go back to sleep. Knowing my luck, he's thought up some kind of new theory about how the Power Rangers came to be, or some other nonsensical shit like that, and he just *has* to discuss it.

"Almost two." The voice is deep, much too deep for my just barely nine-year-old son. I tense up for a moment before the voice speaks again, telling me to relax. It's like a shot to my soul.

Jim.

Everything I felt earlier, from the pure ecstasy of our lovemaking to the embarrassment of being rejected so soon after, rushes forward, and I want to just bury myself in the blankets and hide. He pulls me against his body, making it impossible for me to get away. I don't fight him. Instead, I just lie there and stew. I'm still half-asleep and trying to figure out what's going on here. Ian's birthday party—that Jim threw. Really hot, sensual sex—with Jim. Saying I love you and being rejected—to and then by Jim.

Motherfucker.

And now I'm awake.

"Jim," I say slowly as my brain finally wakes up. Jim Stone is in my bed. He's spooning me. In my bed. In my apartment. My apartment that I didn't invite him into.

"Babe." It's a statement, not an answer.

"You're in my apartment. At two in the morning."

"Yeah, I know. Listen, we gotta go. I already

grabbed some of your and Ian's shit."

My brain is awake now and going a million miles a minute. What the hell does he mean by that?

"Don't ask me any questions. I can't answer them, okay? But we have to go. Do you trust me?"

God help me, but I do. He might have broken my heart, but that doesn't mean I don't trust him. I'm probably an idiot. Slowly, I nod. I can't bring myself to freak out even though I probably should. Maybe freaking out is something normal women do in this situation, so maybe this makes me not normal, but I trust that Jim wouldn't drag me and my boy out of bed in the middle of the night for nothing.

Pulling myself out of the bed, I'm conscious of how I move, careful not to kick my kid. Wait, where is my kid? I'm so tired and half a step from whining, but my mom-gene kicks in, and none of that matters if I don't know where my boy is. When I put him to sleep, he was right beside me. Jim would be worried about Ian, though, wouldn't he? He wouldn't just open the door and let him walk out? I shake my head, dismissing my own crazy. He's nine, and he doesn't sleepwalk. He's fine. I hate being woken up. It's bad enough being woken up by a kid who's way too peppy for his own good every morning, but at two a.m.? No and fuck that. Clearly, my inner drama queen is on high alert when I'm woken up at inappropriate times.

"Damn you're cute," Jim says from the other side of the bed. I blink up at him as he strides toward me and cups my face in his hands. My nose scrunches up in response as I muffle a yawn. "My grouchy girl."

"Shut up," I say. My cheeks heat, and a stupid smile plants itself on my lips. There he goes sweet-talking again. I don't know what's worse—the sweet-talking or the way his eyes bore into mine when he's not sweet-talking. I can't take it. "Where's Ian?"

He nods his head toward the couch and withdraws his hands. I turn my head to find my boy sitting up on the couch, his head tipped back and mouth hanging open like he's trying to catch flies in his sleep. The tension leaves my body immediately. Jim must have moved him from the bed. Ian's always had trouble sleeping and doesn't take to waking up in unfamiliar situations, so the fact that Jim moved him and my kid's fallen right back asleep is a big deal. With a big, stupid grin on my face, I look up at Jim and just hope he knows what he means to us. But in case he doesn't, I grab hold of his leather cut, pull him to me, and press my lips to his. He tries to deepen the kiss, but I pull back and step away. He just rejected me and I'm still all over him. This isn't going to end badly. It's going to end in a fiery crash that destroys me.

"We need to get going," he says, turning away.

"Are we in danger?"

"No," he says quickly but then lets out a heavy sigh. "Remember, you said you'd trust me."

I'm skeptical, but I'm already up and out of bed. I eye Jim as he leans down and scoops my sleeping boy into his arms. The sight of this man cradling my kid like he weighs nothing shuts down my fears. Jim's not like the rest of them. He's not Carlo or Ian's father. He's not the others. He's not perfect, for sure, but maybe he could just be perfect for us. If he wanted me, that is. Ian might not say much about Jim, but he talks about Ryan all the time. Those two are thick as thieves. And this right here? My kid sleeping through a man picking him up means a lot. For the kid who used to go days without sleep and could only eat certain color foods and who had a panic attack every single day to trust Jim enough that he can fall asleep in his arms does me in.

When Jim turns toward the door, I scramble to grab a bra and shove it in the pocket of the hoodie I grab and then slip on a pair of flip flops and follow him to the door. He stops, and I wait behind him awkwardly until he raises an eyebrow and nods at the closed door. I look at my sleeping boy in his arms, who isn't exactly small, and quickly move to open it. Jim walks through the open door and effortlessly carries my boy down the flight of stairs to the sidewalk below. He wastes no time getting Ian tucked safely into the minivan.

I pause a moment before shutting and locking the door behind me, still having no clue what the hell is going on. Jim seemed so earnest that I didn't have the heart to send him away. So without any argument, I make my way down the stairs and into the front passenger seat of the minivan. We ride in silence away from Fort Bragg's small downtown and through one street after another. The drive is probably not nearly as long as it feels, in all honesty. My brain is just not waking up. When I first heard Jim's voice behind me, I felt a jolt of energy that has since worn off in favor of the prospect of taking a nap. After only a few blocks away from Main Street, my eyelids grow heavy and start to force my eyes to close. We could be going anywhere and doing anything, so I need to stay alert, but I can't help my body's inability to muster up the energy to do so.

"No napping for you." Jim's voice laughs from the driver's seat and cuts the engine. "Come on inside before I lose those pretty eyes."

Somehow, through the will of God himself, I manage to pry my eyes open. We're parked in the narrow drive of a small bungalow in town. It's nothing special, with few accents to its exterior, and painted in a dull and fading gray. The lawn is freshly mowed, but the flower beds are empty save for the dirt-mud mix that should be housing the roots of brightly colored flowers. I know the color of the paint despite the time of night and that the flower beds should be filled because this isn't just any cute little bungalow in town. It's Jim's bungalow. For a moment, I don't understand why we're here, but then I realize that of course we'd be here. Ryan isn't in the car with us, and wherever we're going, we need to take him, too. My brain swims with a hundred possibilities. Everything from worrying about Jim leaving a sleeping boy home alone—especially *that* sleeping boy—to what's wrong, and how much danger we're in. I can't even keep up with my own damn thoughts and fears.

"Inside," he says again, this time louder. His voice carries enough that Ian stirs in the backseat. When I don't get moving, Jim goes about extracting himself from the vehicle and then scooping Ian up and walking toward the front door. My brain kicks into gear, and I chase after him, knowing the drill. But he doesn't need me. The front door swings open and out steps Rage. Jim wastes no time slipping into the house with my boy.

Standing on the stoop, Rage stares me down. His black beard has gray streaks and is tamed by a messy braid that he let Nicole try on him. I bite my lip at the memory of this big, mean man letting a tiny little girl braid his beard. Rage has a soft side, and I didn't know it until today. Knowing this about him now, I give him a soft smile and point to the beard. He huffs, a near snarl forming on his lips.

"You're a softie, George Stone."

"Used to like you," he says with a grunt. I close the distance between us and let my smile take over my face. I yawn halfway through, but even the sleepiness can't steal this moment from me. Rage just walks past me and heads for the Harley that I now see is parked on the street.

"You still like me," I say boldly. I don't know that he really likes anyone except for his wife. He must like Sylvia, because she has that huge-ass closet in the cabin he built for their retirement. He probably likes

Jim well enough, since the man made it through childhood and puberty to live until thirty and meet me. I'm thinking he's got to love Ryan, because I don't know a soul alive who wouldn't fall in love with that little punk. But Sylvia and I are tight, and she likes me, so I'm thinking Rage does, too. Or at least that's what I'm choosing to tell myself.

"We'll see."

I stand and watch as Rage mounts his bike and takes off like a light. Only when he disappears around the corner do I let myself in and marvel at the state of Jim's house. I haven't spent a whole hell of a lot of time here, but enough to know that it's probably never been this clean before. There are no empty beer bottles lying around on random surfaces, and none of Ryan's toys are on the floor for me to step on. This place normally looks like a minefield of sharp objects and old food. I don't know what the occasion is, but I like it.

The house is made up of the average-sized living room that looks over an L-shaped kitchen and small dining area. On the other side of the house is a short hallway with a small hall bath and two rooms just big enough to not be small, with two shallow linen closets set on either side of the bathroom. With Jim nowhere in sight, I let my curiosity get the better of me and I sneak into the kitchen. There's not a lot of storage space in here, but enough for what few dishes Jim has. Normally the cabinets are pretty barren, but as I poke around, I find that they're full. Full of dishes and serving platters. Full of boxes of food and plastic storage containers. There's so much *stuff* that all that space I thought this kitchen had is nonexistent. Even the fridge is full of food. Real food that's used to create meals, not just beer and cheese sticks with the occasional expired luncheon meat.

"Either you're looking for leftover cake, or you're trying to figure out where I hid all the debris from the floor," Jim says. I jump in place, right myself, and slam the fridge door shut. Shit, busted. When I turn around, my cheeks are red, and I'm doing my best to meet Jim's eyes. I'm not normally shy, but we've had sex, and I'm kind of totally in love with this man, and he's arching one of his brows in this faux judgmental manner than makes my stupid tired brain kind of hot.

"I found the leftover cake—second shelf. The debris is still MIA, though," I say.

"You ran out on me." He walks toward me and stares down into my eyes with a fierceness that I'm really not used to.

"You had to go home," I say. I mean, that's what happened, isn't it? Or did I get my signals crossed?

Jim brings his face down to my level and shakes his head. He smiles as he says, "No, *we* had to get home. But *you* didn't give me a chance to explain."

His explanation makes sense, but I don't feel it in my soul the way I felt the words he spoke earlier. I'm left with the impression that he feels obligated to do this stuff for me and my son. It's like he thinks because I do a lot for and with Ryan that he has to somehow make it even with Ian. He doesn't. Nothing's worse than pity, but being somebody's obligation is a close second. I've been an obligation, and I don't like it. I want to be somebody's option instead.

"You don't have to do this."

"What's that, momma?"

I repeat myself, only louder this time. He stares at me incredulously before taking my hand and silently dragging me out of the kitchen and down the hall to Ryan's bedroom. He opens the closed door slowly and cringes when it squeaks, then gestures for me to go in. I assume the boys are passed out on Ryan's bed, but that's not what I find at all.

Ryan's bedroom used to make the living room look like it'd been visited by a maid. He had a twin bed with a single dresser and a toy chest that was always closed but also always empty. All the toys were on the floor. Half his clothes were in a pile near the closet, and the clean ones were usually half hanging out of open dresser drawers. But that's not what I'm seeing now. The miniature window blinds are half-open, allowing a stream of light to come in from the street and giving me enough visibility to really look around. In the corner of the room, a new set of bright red, metal bunk beds takes place of the old twin. My attention is fixed on my boy, sprawled out like he hasn't a care in the world on the bottom bunk, only half-covered with the action-figure comforter. Not just any action figure, but his favorite action figure graces the comforter, pillow, and sheets he's lying on. I take a few steps into the room to find that Ryan, on the top bunk, is curled up under a similar bed set with his favorite superhero's cartoon likeness printed all over it.

"I don't understand," I whisper. Jim's presence looms behind me, simultaneously taking up space and making me feel safe and protected. It's a dangerous feeling. I could get used to this.

"I said we have to get *home*."

Jim's words sink in slowly as I take in the rest of the space. A second dresser sits next to Ryan's. It's a little newer-looking, but not by much. Above each dresser is a metal placard that's almost the shape of a license plate.

One has Ryan's name stamped into the metal.

The other has Ian's.

I gasp, but before I can say anything that would wake the boys, Jim leads me out of the room. Is he moving us in? What the hell is he doing? He can't really be moving us in. That's crazy. Back down the hallway and through the open doorway of his bedroom, we make our way to a private space that's ripe with possibilities.

I'm pretty much dead on my feet, but the prospect of being with Jim again has me alert in a way that nothing else tonight has been able to do. Jim's room, just like the other rooms, is clean. I'm not surprised by it, but rather grateful. I want to fall into Jim's bed and make love until we pass out. Or just pass out. I could honestly go for either right now. All the while my internal monologue is contemplating whether or not I have enough energy to have sex, Jim's been closing the door, making note of the working lock, and shedding himself of his clothes. The leather vest goes on the back of a nearby chair. The rest of his clothes, save for his boxers, get tossed onto the floor. When he's done, he starts to work on my clothes. I could fight, but a sexy, mostly naked man I love is stripping me when I'm dog tired. There is literally no way I could manage to pitch a fit right now.

"Now, you listen good," he says as he frees me from my slip-on shoes. "I don't ever feel like I have to do something, except maybe listening to my fucking father in Church. I know the men in your past never did treat you good, the way you deserve, but I'm not them. I tell you that you're it for me and my kid, I fucking mean it. You're the kind of woman that men bleed for, the kind that men bleed other men over. You're a great mom, not just to your kid, but to mine, too. I told you earlier that I remember every detail of the day I met you, and it didn't seem to make a fucking difference."

I'm down to my panties—a fresh pair that are also decidedly unsexy and almost as worn as the last pair he saw—and my pajama top. There wasn't a whole lot to undress considering the two a.m. pseudo-kidnapping he masterminded. Jim's hands trail up my bare legs and rest beneath my shirt, on my hips, above my panty line.

"Woman, you must be off your fucking rocker if you thought I was gonna tell you I love you for the first time while my dick's wet. I had a plan, and your horny ass ruined it. I set this place up, had some of the lost girls get it clean, and was going to bring you back here after the party. *Then* I was gonna tell you I love you, and *then* I was gonna get my dick wet. You fucked up the order of operations, babe."

"You had a plan." It's a statement, not a question.

"Yeah, you think I did all this shit for me and the boy? Please. He's the one who told me you'd never agree to live with us if we didn't clean it up."

"You want us to live with you." I blink, not sure what to say. I want to live with him. I want everything with him. I'm also stupid and impulsive, and I do things I regret later, so my judgment is questionable at best.

"I love you, momma. Have since the moment I laid eyes on you. Just had to get rid of the competition first."

"Competition?"

"The boy. For a nine-year-old, he's really fucking smooth."

"I do love that boy," I muse, finally resurrecting my speaking abilities. "Wait. You love me?"

"Don't be stupid," he says. "You're mine now. The club knows it. You know it. Our boys know it."

"I don't know what to say." This is the fairy tale that happens to good girls who have virtue and modesty. The good girls who never whored themselves out or slept with their sister's husband. This is the kind of speech a woman like me doesn't deserve. But he's giving it to me anyway. For some reason, this imperfect, misguided, beautiful man wants me. He knows my darkness, and he still wants me. I can't let that go no matter how much I fear that kind of blind loyalty and commitment.

"Say thank you," he says. Breathing heavily, he pulls me against him and shoves his face in the crook of my neck. I gasp but don't speak. He repeats himself. The least I can do is acquiesce.

"Thank you." My chest is heaving, and my hands shake, but I grip him tight against me. I love him. I love him in a way that's unhealthy. Obsessive. Needy. This man is more than trouble. He's a goddamn tornado waiting to touch down. He could destroy me—if I let him.

CHAPTER FIFTEEN

September 28, 1997

I hate days like today. They are the absolute worst, but if I'm being honest with myself it's not "days like today" that are the problem. It's today. September 28. Today the twins turn three. I can't believe it's been that long since I brought them into this world. Two years, ten months, and seventeen days since I last held them in my arms. And it's still so fresh. Sometimes when I close my eyes, I swear I can smell them. Even after all this time. I don't think a mother forgets something like that.

Cease (the Bayonet Scars finale)

The pain seems worse this year. Maybe it's because this time last year I was already completely miserable. The only thing I had to live for was Ian. Now I have Jim and Ryan, and Ian has them, too. And by extension, the entire Forsaken family, which is large and protective. It's a lot of people to be grateful for. And I *am* grateful for them. It's just that nothing and no one can take this pain away. And I don't really think they should. A mother shouldn't be able to turn off the pain of losing her kids. Selfishly, I wonder if the pain is worse when your babies are dead. Like, they're not out living and loving on another woman, thinking that's their mom. Does that make it better? Would it make it better if it weren't my own sister who they cry for?

I don't think anything is better or worse than this, if I'm being honest. Except maybe death itself. And because of that, I keep my babies close and don't talk about them much. Only my guys know that today is their birthday, and I like it that way. We had to explain the babies to Ryan a few months ago, and that was hard in itself. He didn't quite understand why we can't just go and get them. The kid even went so far as to say we could "just take care of it" in a way that left me unsettled to say the least. I didn't even tell Sylvia what today is. She knows about the babies and all, but she's got enough going on with the chemo. It seems wrong, somehow, to tell too many people, like the more people I tell about them, the less they really belong to me. I shared Ian with Jim, and now he's not entirely just mine anymore. And I'm trying to be okay with that, even though the last couple of months have proven to me that when Jim Stone says he is all in, he is all fucking in.

But this—this is too much.

I brought Ian in the bedroom with me for a little bit this morning before Jim took him and Ryan into the kitchen for breakfast. I just had to check in and make sure he's okay. The regular school year started last month, and Ian's only had one freak-out in class, which is a huge improvement over summer school. He hasn't wet the bed in the middle of the night in a few weeks, and he won't let me carry him anymore. Jim got Ian in with Ryan's pediatrician, and she's been great. I think the boys have a little crush on her, and if I'm being honest, I do, too. I've never once felt judged by her, and she's made it a point to work with the school psychologist to get my boy to vocalize his needs more. Still, despite all his progress, I still see the fear in my little boy's eyes. He's waiting for the other shoe to drop. And last week a kid asked him and Ryan why Jim and I aren't married and said they're not really brothers unless we're married.

Trying to explain adult relationships to a nine-year-old boy was difficult at best. He still doesn't understand, and I can't bring myself to say anything to Jim.

Jim's good to me. And I'm grateful. Just like I'm grateful for everything I have in my life. If I look back at where I was even six months ago, I can see how much better everything is. It used to be months would go by with me feeling like this all the time. Like dying. Like maybe if my little boy had somebody else to live for him, then I wouldn't have to do it anymore. He does, actually. So I could be done, if I really wanted to be. But Jim has no legal rights to Ian, so even though he'd be better off without me, I know the system. I know what they do to kids with special needs like my boy. They'd contact his biological father since he's on the birth certificate. Best case scenario, that asshole doesn't show up and my kid ends up in foster care. With his issues? Nobody would adopt him. Worst case scenario, that piece of shit who knocked me up at sixteen when he was nearly thirty takes my kid in. I know nothing about that fucker, and I don't want to know anything about him either.

There were days in the not-so-distant past where I wasn't sure I could take another breath, because breathing was too painful. I never wanted Ian to suffer, but for a long time, suffering was only thing I gave him. The realization that I'm the only one he has was literally the only thing that kept me alive for the better part of the last few years. And now? I have two boys. And on normal days, I let myself believe that they're both mine. I love Ryan just as much as I love Ian. They both need me, just in different ways. Still, today I feel like loving this little boy will only lead me to a broken heart. And I can't lose another child.

Okay, that's it. This pity party needs to end. Maybe if I just turn enough to my side, I might be able to smother myself with my own pillow. I'm even on my own nerves at this point. I just don't know how to feel it any less dramatically. I don't know how to let myself grieve my babies without being all end-of-the-world and doom-and-gloom about it. It consumes me, but the pain is a welcome reminder that I haven't forgotten them and that I don't love them any less than I did the day they were born. That I don't miss them any less than the day I lost them.

"You better be eating your food," Jim hollers from behind the closed bedroom door, his voice carrying as he walks down the hall. He made me bacon and eggs for breakfast. That was hours ago, though, and I still haven't touched them. Ryan snuck in to give me a rare kiss a little while ago and managed to walk out with a fist full of bacon. It was the only thing that made me laugh all day. Ian normally tries to cheer me up when I'm sad, but he knows what today is, and he couldn't bring himself to try. Up until about a year ago, he used to tell me that he misses his baby sister and brother. He used to say he wanted to teach Michael how to ride a bike and that he wishes he could hold Alexandra one more time.

"Answer me, babe."

I try to respond, but nothing comes out. Today is the first time Jim's ever seen me like this—near catatonic. Part of me hopes this is going to be the first and last time. But then, I also hope it isn't. I hate feeling crazy, but I can't ever feel like I don't care about my babies anymore.

The door creaks open, and Jim stares at me through the small crack between the door and frame. His eyes are sad, but the smile on his lips tries to hide it. He closes the door a moment later and shouts at the boys to get ready to leave. I don't know where they're going, and he doesn't bother to tell me. After breakfast, he announced that they'd be playing video games in the living room. And later, he let me know they'd be in the backyard working on their fighting skills. Grady had come by to help Jim with giving the boys tips. This is their thing—it's important to Jim that he teach our boys how to defend themselves. Judging by the moves I've seen previously, Jim had already taught Ryan a few things, so I suspect this is more for Ian than anything. I'd say it's a kind gesture, but it's not. This is just who Jim is when he's not drinking himself stupid and snorting shit that makes him act like somebody he's not. The thought makes me burst into tears again.

Eventually I stop crying and give up on trying to sleep, so I go for just staring up at the ceiling and trying to make patterns out of the popcorn texture. I don't know how long I lie there for. I just know that the boys leave and come back and then leave again for dinner at Chief's house with his family. Before they left, the boys brought me snack cakes, and Jim forced me to sit up enough to drink water. I didn't want it, but he held my nose closed until I had to draw a breath and inadvertently sucked in some water. Bastard. It hurt going down, and I mentally cussed him out for nearly an hour. At some point, I managed to reason with myself. Jim was doing it to help me, not hurt me, and so I took back all those curses I put on his dick. Even knowing that he's taking care of me, I still can't bring myself to not hate him and everything in this world except those four kids that mean more to me than my own life.

When they return after dinner, Jim pulls me up and forces me to drink water again. I lie loose in his arms, letting him support my weight, and I fight swallowing until he says the only thing that can get through to me. "You're scaring our boys, Ian especially. I've tried to keep him out of here so he doesn't have to see you like this, but it's not easy. Elle asked where you were tonight, and when Ryan shot his mouth off, telling the entire table why, Ian ran from the table. It took me thirty minutes to get him to come out of the bathroom, and when he did, he'd scratched the shit out of his arms and neck. You need to pull your shit together, because I'm doing all I can here, but it's not enough. He needs you."

When the sting of his honesty subsides, I take a sip of water, and it feels so good to my parched throat that I gulp down the rest of the glass greedily. When I'm done, Jim places the glass on the bedside table. We stay like that for a few minutes before I force myself up from the bed. Jim gives me space as I change and wash my face and even brush my hair. I have my hand on the doorknob before he speaks again.

"Those kids, they're not dirty little secrets. You

don't have two kids—you have four. Three boys and one girl. Next year, we buy a cake and celebrate their birthday even if they're not here with us. On Christmas, we hang their stockings, buy them presents—even if those presents go to the shelter after—and we make damn sure this year doesn't repeat itself. Our sons deserve to know those babies exist. They have every right to share in their mother's pain. You don't shut us out. Next time you need a time out, just say so, and we'll head out. But not on days when Ian and Ryan need you. Got that?"

My eyes fall closed, but no tears fall. I'm literally out of juice, so I just nod my agreement. Jim comes up behind me, wrapping me in a hug, and kisses the top of my head.

"Sorry you're hurting, babe. You need something, we'll get you to a doctor. But I can't do this alone. Ian needs his mom."

"I know," I say and leave the room to go pretend to be happy with my boys.

CHAPTER SIXTEEN

March 1998

"Mom!"

The scream that comes from the boy's room is deafening. The knife in my hand stills while I wait to see if this is one of those situations I really do need to go in there for. Ryan's ten now—he just had his birthday last week. In an effort to avoid getting in trouble as often as he does, he informed me that I only need to show up if I've been called three times in a row. Apparently, if I show up after the first time Ian calls for me, the boy doesn't even get a swing in.

According to Ryan, that's not fair. But this is Ryan's screams, not Ian's. It didn't used to be like this. It used to be Ian crying and screaming for help, but ever since I gave in and let Jim teach the boys how to fight, Ian's been coming out on top more often. I'd be lying if I said it didn't make me proud. A few months ago, Ian started karate at the local rec center. Ryan lasted three classes before their sensei said he was too unruly to teach, but Ian's absolutely flourished in the classes. He started with his white belt, progressed to blue pretty quickly, and is on the verge of getting his purple belt. He's been working super hard for it, but it's not been easy. It's worth it, though. Marital arts is giving my kid a sense of power and control that seems to be healing him.

"Mom! Help! Mom!" Ryan's screaming again. With a sigh, I set down the knife and eye the pile of tomatoes I have yet to chop. I'm not sure how Rage convinced me to make the salsa for this weekend's upcoming barbecue, but he did. I like making salsa, don't get me wrong. But making salsa for four is a hell of a lot different than making salsa for over fifty people, half of which have stupidly large appetites.

"Um, Mom?" Ian's voice breaks through my thoughts now. It's tentative and loaded with probably about fifty bucks' worth of damage. Their room looked so nice when we first moved in. A few weeks later and it was officially broken in as the bedroom of two rowdy boys. Two rowdy boys who seriously don't understand the concept of "you break it, you buy it." So I take my time washing and drying my hands. They broke something, I already know it. And it's going to cost Jim money one way or another. I'm just hoping it's not another bone. My boys are tough as all get out until they're laid up on the couch, unable to move, and then it's like they're complete invalids. Broken arms I can deal with a lot better than broken legs. If it's a broken leg, I'm going to stay with Sylvia and Rage until it heals.

"I should go." I'm talking to myself aloud now. It might make me crazy, but it's not the first time I've been accused of such, so I go with it. "Good moms run to their kids' aide. They don't hide out in the kitchen, stalling."

"I don't think she's coming," Ryan says. He's shouting it, making damn sure I hear. Neither boy is bothering to come out, and they're not crying, so I know they're not in a lot of pain.

Ian speaks up, defending me like any good son should, saying, "She's not just going to leave us here."

I love that boy. As a nod to his faith in me, I walk to the fridge, pull out a beer, pop the top, and take a swig. I won't actually leave them there, but I'm not going to run to their aide either. They're not little boys anymore, and they don't get into little trouble, so they can learn to wait it out. I continue to enjoy my beer as they place bets on whether or not I'm going to come to their rescue.

"This is a very not-mom thing to do, lady," Ryan shouts. I snicker and shake my head while giving myself a mental pat on the back. Just when I'm feeling more mom-guilt than I can handle, I set down the beer and head for the hallway.

The loud rumble of Jim's bike sounds in the distance, growing nearer every second. I let out a relieved breath. If dad's home, I can be the good cop and cuddle my babies for their stupidity. That's why I hate handling things solo so much. I don't have anyone to pawn the responsibility of the discipline off on.

"Dad's coming! Shit!" Ryan shouts, now sounding panicked. Oh, whatever they did is good. Real good. I want to be mad, but I can't bring myself to.

As of today, Ian and I have officially been in Fort

Bragg for one year. And our lives are so completely different than they were before. My boy has a home and a brother. He even has a dad. I still have my moments of doubt, of this sinking fear that all of this will end, but then Jim reminds me of who he is. Not just with the promises he makes, but the things he does. The reminder is there, in every single touch and every sly smile he gives me. It's in the lingering looks, like he wants to tell me something but not quite ready to just yet.

    I gave up thinking those looks meant that he wanted to make this thing between us legal months ago. The one time I asked him it was way too early in our relationship. Ryan had just called me "Mom" for the first time, so I was riding that high, and it just came out. It was right after Thanksgiving, and I was so grateful for everything I now have and also so incredible guilty over almost forgetting about Alexandra and Michael. It was just this split second, where I was basting the turkey and I thought, *I have everything I ever wanted*. It was a sharp, painful reminder of what I don't have. My twins. My babies aren't here, so how could I, even for a fucking second, think I have everything? I just stopped what I was doing, left the room, and curled into a ball on our bed, drowning in my own tears. Jim came in and tried to make it better, but he didn't know how and soon came to realize he couldn't. It was a slow realization for him—deep in his heart, he still thinks he can get my babies back. They're not even babies anymore. This past September, they turned three. I wonder about their hair color and their eyes. I wonder how their personalities have developed, and selfishly, I pray to nothing in particular that they remember me. That somehow, those first few weeks with them meant enough that they'd recognize me somehow if they saw me. And it was too much, far too overwhelming. I couldn't handle it and was just looking for something to make me feel better. So when I was able to speak, I just blurted it out. "Do you even want to marry me?" All he said was, "Can't," and then crawled out of bed and disappeared until dinner time when there were too many people around to talk about it. He hasn't brought it up since and neither have I. It was greedy of me to even suggest it. He's already given us so much.

The back door creaks open behind me, followed by heavy boots against the laminate flooring. One deep breath after another and I'm halfway to looking like a normal person. I don't want Jim seeing me like this. We're doing good. There's no reason to bring us down with my baggage.

"What's wrong, momma?" His voice comes from a few feet behind me. He hasn't even seen my face yet, and he already knows. He has this uncanny sense about him. He always knows, and I always think I can fool him. Instead of saying a word, I just point in the direction of the boys' bedroom. Crappy mom point two—throwing the kids under the bus to save myself.

"What did they do?" Each word he speaks is punctuated with his annoyance, but he doesn't stomp toward their room like I expect. Instead, he wraps his arms around me from behind and pulls me against his chest. "I'll take care of them in a minute, but first I want to know what's wrong."

"You know what's wrong," I say. My eyes fall closed, and I sink into my man. Jim's chest is firm, even more built than when I met him a year ago. He doesn't drink as much or do as many drugs as he used to. We have an agreement. He can do whatever he wants as long as he can keep his shit together, and if he gets too out of hand, I let him know. So far we've only had two situations arise, and even though he was a real bastard the first time we went through it, he found out the hard way that we wouldn't be having an issue like that again. And we haven't. The second time he partied too hard and I had to rein him in, he didn't give me any shit. Because that's who we are as a couple.

It's a long while before he says anything, because that's how he is. With everybody else, Jim shoots his mouth off before thinking, but with me he's careful and considerate. At least he is now.

"It's okay to be sad, momma." He gives me a squeeze, and his hands travel down from just beneath my breasts to my belly. It'll never be flat after three kids, but it's not as chunky as it used to be. There's still stretch marks and scars from the twins' birth—marks that Jim's studied and traced. With one hand, he palms my belly. I hate the gesture even though I know it's coming from a good place.

"Carried those babies for almost nine full months. You know them in a way nobody else ever will, and the way Mancuso stole them from you? That shit is fucked. I can't make that right the way I want to, but I can promise you that I'm never going to stop trying, and that means if you gotta cry or be sad, you just fucking do it."

Tears fall down my cheeks no matter how hard I squeeze my eyes shut to try to stop them. Jim hates the tears. He doesn't exactly recoil, but I know that he doesn't know what to do with me when I'm crying. The man with all the answers always goes radio silent.

"We good?"

I nod my head in response and take a deep breath as the tears dry up.

"Now, what did the boys do to piss you off?"

"Oh fuck," I shout and push off from Jim and rush across the room. I forgot about the boys. I forgot about my children, and they could be missing a leg or bleeding out or... oh my God... they could be dead.

"Babe, you want my dick, all you have to do is say so." Jim chases after me and shouts in confusion when I go down the hall in the opposite direction he expects.

I burst through the boys' closed bedroom door and stop in my tracks. Jim's moving so close behind, he slams into my back and has to grab hold of me so I don't fall over.

"Well, it's about time," Ryan says with a sigh.

Ian's brown eyes stare at me, loaded with judgment and disappointment. He shakes his head and says, "I expected better of you."

The furniture is all in place, and neither boy appears to be bleeding. Clearly, both of their mouths work just fine.

"You," Jim says, pointing a finger at Ian. "Start talking."

"We were watching *E.T.*, and it was all Ian's idea," Ryan says. He shifts in place uncomfortably and pulls away from Ian a little before righting himself. They're standing awful close. Shoulder to shoulder close. Neither seems very happy about it, but they're purposefully not moving.

"And?" Jim's voice is hard and brokers no argument from either boy. I take a step forward to allow Jim into the room and watch as he approaches the kids. Ryan's eyes dart from mine to his dad's and back again. His big gray orbs scream "help me," but I just shrug my shoulders and act like there's nothing I can do. Ian, on the other hand, is staring Jim straight in the eyes. The kid doesn't even look remorseful or like he's in the least bit of trouble. Christ, maybe all those karate classes aren't so good for him after all. He used to at least be fearful of our disapproval.

"Son," Jim says, focusing on Ian. He bends down to meet his eyes and waits. The boys exchange a few looks before Ian steps away from Ryan. Despite the distance between their bodies, their lower arms are still firmly attached. Jim reaches out, taking each of their arms in a hand and tries to pull them apart. Both Ian and Ryan wince in discomfort.

"Are you fucking kidding me?" Jim says, trying to separate their arms again. Still, they don't budge.

"Babe, your kids Super Glue'd their arms together," I say, now eyeing the small tube lying on the floor near Ryan's feet.

Jim snorts and shakes his head before falling to his ass. His shoulders shake as he strains for breath. His face turns red, and the sounds of his fucking cackling can probably be heard all the way to the beach. I bite my lip, doing my best to keep a straight face. Neither boy knows what to do with their dad, and honestly neither do I.

"Today?" he says, eyeing Ian. "You choose today of all days?"

Our boy just shrugs in answer.

"No, seriously. Your grandparents are going to be pissed."

"Why would they care? They're not the ones who have to deal with this mess," I say as I step forward and examine their glued-together skin.

"Actually, they are," Jim says with a smirk. "We're going on a ride. Get these two assholes packed up for a sleepover."

"But we can't," I say in desperate realization that their arms are glued together from the wrist to the elbow. Jesus fuck. Sylvia finished her last round of chemo a few weeks back, and she's still not feeling great. I know she loves having the kids around, but that doesn't mean she can handle dealing with this disaster. And Rage, well, he's likely to leave my kids attached like this for us to deal with upon our return from wherever Jim thinks we're going.

"Yeah, Dad. Looks like I get Mom tonight," Ryan says in a smug as fuck tone. He then turns his attention to me, and with big gray eyes, he says, "It kind of hurts."

"I'm sure it does, you little con artist. Pack your own bags. We're dropping you off at Grandma's in twenty." And with that, I walk out of the room and back to the kitchen where I finish my beer and then grab another from the fridge. I love my kids, but Jesus fuck, I could use a night off.

CHAPTER SEVENTEEN

Dropping the boys off at Rage and Sylvia's wasn't fun. Neither was driving them there. First, it took them over half an hour to pack. Ian started whining at some point, and Jim tried to help, but I shut that down real quick. If my boys are stupid enough to Super Glue their arms together, then they can figure out how to work together long enough to pack an overnight bag. Then getting them into the van was another feat, but not nearly as difficult as getting them out was. Still, there was a certain kind of sweetness in seeing the look on Rage's face and hearing his disgruntled promise to get the glue situation taken care of. Sylvia was napping when we got there. Now, as we quietly make out way out of the cabin and toward Jim's bike, I'm grateful that she's still sleeping. She needs her rest, and I can only hope that Rage figures out how to solve that glue issue without having to drag her into it.

"So, where are we going and how long have you been planning this?" I've waited long enough to ask the questions, knowing that Jim only answers when he's good and ready.

"Can't tell you," he says. He climbs on his bike first and puts up the kickstand. I climb on right after him. He revs the engine and drives us through the tall pines toward the road. But just when we're about to turn that direction, Jim stalls the bike.

Shouting over the engine, he says, "Babe, look at that."

I follow the line of his outstretched finger and eye the sight before me. It's gorgeous. Rage and Sylvia's little cabin is surrounded by a nest of pine trees that shields the cabin from the noise from the road. Jim turns the opposite direction and rides through the narrow tree line to the plot behind the cabin. We've never been over here, had no reason to be, but I'm strangely excited about exploring the land. I'm not exactly sure how far back Rage and Sylvia's property goes, but I know the cabin is well insulated.

Just beyond the trees, a large field awaits us. On the right side, the tree line extends as far as my eyes can see. The rest is wide open save for an old red barn that sits off to the left side. Jim pauses the Harley before we ride over an old, worn bridge. I hold my breath and hang on tight with my eyes scrunched closed. I've never been a fan of bridges, especially not old rickety ones that I doubt have been cared for in the last twenty years. It's one of those structures that probably wasn't ever in very good shape, and now we're taking a several-hundred-pound machine across it like it's nothing.

When I open my eyes, we're well across the bridge and into the field. There are pockets of little hills and valleys, making it a bumpy ride. But by the time my stomach starts to feel uneasy, we're past it—just like the bridge, my anxiety about the rough terrain outlasts the terrain itself—and onto a smooth ride through a lush grassy-green field. It's March now, and the winter's rainy season has only barely just let up, leaving a wealth of thriving plants behind. I wasn't sure how I'd take to Fort Bragg at first, with it being so cold and rainy so much of the year, but now that I'm here, I can't imagine living anywhere else.

Right in the middle of the plot of land, just a few

yards from the barn, Jim brings the bike to a stop. In the distance, near a dirt road, I can barely make out a sign. It looks like the land is for sale or has been sold. Or maybe it's a sign letting everybody know that something's going to be built here. I can't really tell.

We climb off and survey the property. It's huge, or at least that's how it feels to me. I grew up first in New York and then was sent to Florida when good old Mom and Dad decided that parenting was better suited to my and Esmeralda's maternal grandparents. Our place in New York was a small little flat in a questionable neighborhood of Queens. My grandparents' house in Florida was a ranch no bigger than the house Jim and I live in now. I can't imagine having this much space to call my own.

"You look happy," Jim says as he comes to stand behind me. He tucks me into his chest and rests his chin atop my head.

"It's peaceful out here. Quiet. I like quiet."

He laughs at my response, his joy radiating through the shaking of his chest against my back. "Yeah it is. If I was stuck at home with a couple of idiots who glue themselves together, I'd want a little patch of quiet, too."

"No, seriously. How does that happen?" The question is rhetorical. We've been over this time and time again, and neither of us actually have an answer for what the fuck is wrong with our kids. We've already banned a variety of different chemicals and items in our house in an effort to keep the place from being lit on fire and destroyed from the roof down.

"You know, I thought Ryan was bad on his own, but Ian really gets him going," Jim says, placing a kiss to the side of my head just above my ear.

"Are you blaming my boy?"

The second the words leave my mouth, I tense up. Ian's not my boy—he's our boy. That's one fight Jim and I had shortly after we moved into the house. He got to being pissed about something and took it out on Ryan, and I kind of lost my cool on him, telling him not to talk to my kids like that. He wasn't even pissed that I said Ryan was mine. He was pissed that I'd been saying it for a while but never gave him the same leeway with Ian. It's unfair, and I know it. The difference is that I know I'm always going to be here for Ryan. I'm always going to mother him and love on him. I love Jim, and I want to believe in what we have, but I have a lifetime of experiences of men lying and changing their minds behind me to make it hard to believe even the most well-intentioned of people.

"Our boy," I correct myself.

"Our boy," he says. His tone is gentle, hopeful even. I know that's all he really wants—for me to trust him with my son the way he trusts me with his. And maybe one day I will.

"It's pretty out here." The sun is nowhere near setting, but it's low enough in the sky for the land to bask in a gorgeous yellow and orange light. Jim didn't pawn the boys off on his parents so we could stand in an empty field, so I try to find a way to get my feet to move. My man had plans for us, and the least I can do is not fuck them up for him.

"Dad put this place up for sale." *Dad*. It's not often that he refers to Rage as his dad, but I hold tight to those moments every time he does.

"Whoever buys it is going to be damn lucky," I say. I want to change the subject, but I don't exactly know why. It's just a piece of land, and it's more than I can afford. I don't know anything about owning land, but all of a sudden, I want it. I want to be on the other side of a tree line from his parents. I want my boys to be able to run over to Grandma's. I want Grandpa close enough to whoop their asses when Jim's not around and they need it. Mostly, I just want some kind of permanency in my life. No matter the amazing things my man says, I still don't feel rooted here. Maybe I'm being pushy, but I need that shit. I need the paper and the deed. I need to know that these kids belong to me and this man isn't going anywhere. I need to know the place where I live has my name on it. I need all of that, and maybe I should be apologizing for being such a needy bitch, but I won't. If Jim's taught me anything in the last year, it's that it's okay to ask for what you want. I just have to find my voice first.

"What if we bought it?"

I'm stunned in silence at his casual suggestion. Pulling my brain out of self-pity mode for a moment, I try to really listen to what he's said to me. His dad put the place up for sale. A little bit of the tension that's been building leaves my body. This land already belongs to the Stone family. We could buy it. But then we'd be living together on a piece of land either he or I—or both of us—own, and we'd still not have the permanency that being married would provide. So, no, I don't want to buy this land from his dad. I don't want any of it unless I can have all of it.

"And what? The deed will say James Stone and Ruby Buckley. Or maybe just James Stone."

Jim pulls away and walks around to face me. His jaw ticks.

"This again?"

"What do you mean 'this again'? I brought up getting married *once* and only once. Don't make me feel bad for doing exactly what you've been encouraging me to do."

"You're half a step from pissing me off." His words are cold and callous in a way I'm no longer used to. Unable to stop myself, I flinch in response but refuse to back down.

"Welcome to the fucking party, Jim. I've been pissed off since Thanksgiving." The longer I stew on my rejected marriage proposal, the more bitter I get. He says he loves me, even says he'll walk through fire, burn the world to the ground, and put up with my fucking crying because I'm it for him. But he won't marry me, and he won't tell me why, so how much of that is bullshit?

"Think I don't know that? You think I *like*

everybody asking when I'm gonna lock you down and not being able to tell them why I haven't already? Newsflash, babe. I. Fucking. Don't. I hear the fucking comments you make to my mother about Grady being married to a junkie. Because, hey, at least they're fucking married, right? I hear it in your goddamn voice when you talk about wanting to adopt Ryan, and I want that for you and him. And I want Ian as mine, but I can't right now, so just fucking let it go."

"Tell me. Tell me why." I'm shouting now, unable to contain my anger. Those fucking tears he talks about are threatening to fall down my cheeks. I won't give him that, though. I won't let Jim reduce me to tears. *Again.* Every time I cry, he holds me and tells me something ridiculous our boys did to distract me from whatever we were fighting about to begin with. And it works almost every time, but not this time. I won't be deterred.

"Can't." His jaw ticks in response. The truth is on the tip of his tongue, and I'm going to get it out of him even if I have to cut the damn appendage out of his mouth myself.

"Tell me," I scream. "Tell me what is so fucking wrong with me. Right now. You don't, Ian and I are gone." Quickly, I scrub my face with my hands and scream into them. I don't mean it. I can't rip Ian away from Ryan and Jim. This is the exact fucking reason I didn't want to get involved with him to begin with. This isn't just about me. I'm trying to protect Ian by forcing the issue, but I might end up taking his family away if I can't get my mouth to shut up and soon.

"Last year, what's one of the first things you told me?" Now he's the one who's screaming. When I don't answer, Jim steps closer, his chest practically pressing into mine. His face is tilted down, and his nostrils flare in anger. "You told me Ian had to trust me. I spent months fucking up before I got that message. There is no you without that boy. Since the day I woke the fuck up and realized that, I've spent every fucking day making sure that kid knows I'm here and he can rely on me."

"So if Ian matters so much to you, why the fuck won't you marry his mother?" Jim using my kid against me has my heart rate spiking. Adrenaline rushes through me, and I push him away from me, but he comes right back, crowding my personal space.

"One fucking week. You couldn't save this shit for another fucking week?" He grabs me by the back of my neck and pulls my face up to meet his. We're so close, our noses brush and our faces heat from the warmth of our breath.

"No, I can't," I say, grinding my teeth in the process.

"Asked our boy what he thought of you two moving in, he was all for it. Couple weeks later, asked him what he thought of us getting married. Little fucker said no. Not until he gets his purple belt. Which he gets next. Fucking. Week."

"What the hell are you even babbling about?" My anger is receding now. What the hell does Ian's karate classes have to do with Jim not wanting to marry me?

Releasing my neck, Jim steps back and fishes his wallet out of his back pocket. He grips a small, worn piece of paper in his hand and stares at it as he puts his wallet back with the other. With a condescending flip of his wrist, he tosses the piece of paper at me and walks away. Once I manage to stop shooting daggers at his back, I retrieve the paper from the grass and unfold it. In bright red crayon, Ian's written out what looks like a contract. The top line reads, "Dad's promise," and right below it, in Jim's writing in black ink, it lays out the promise he's made to Ian. "I, Dad, won't ask Mom to marry me until Ian has his purple belt." Those fucking tears are back, and they're welling in my eyes. Off to the side, shoved in the corner, is an amendment to the agreement that stipulates that Ryan agrees if he and Ian both get new bikes and that video game system I hate so much that all three of my guys are addicted to. Jim's signature sits next to a bright red X, while Ian and Ryan's are written in red and black crayon, respectively, beneath that. In small writing that's almost too difficult to read, Ryan's written, "Don't tell her. Make her sweat," in black crayon. The note is dated from October. My man's been carrying this little piece of paper around with him, keeping a promise and a secret that he could have easily broken, since October. Holy shit.

"You want to marry me?" I choke the words out, barely able to contain the emotion.

Slowly, with a grim smile on his face, Jim stalks back toward me.

"What do you think?"

"You really want to marry me?"

He's standing in front of me again. This time, his anger is gone, but his expression isn't relieved.

"I just broke the trust of both my sons," he says.

"Ryan's just a shit. He wants me to ask you in front of him. Because this is a packaged deal and all. Ian just needs to know I won't run. He needs to know I'm not going to hurt him or you. He has to trust me, and I can't get him to trust me if you force my hand and make me tell you everything."

"But you *do* want to marry me?"

"Yes. Fuck. Christ, yeah. I've wanted to marry you since the night I made VP. I've wanted to fuck you since the moment I met you. I've known that this thing between us was going to be for-fucking-ever since the moment you handed me my ass because I wasn't being the kind of dad our boys deserve. And I was going to take you on a fucking ride today and give you some grand fucking speech about marrying your bitchy ass one day."

"Okay."

"Say you're sorry," he says.

I shake my head and clear my throat. "I had reason to be pissed," I say. I probably should apologize, but my man wants to marry me. He wants to make us a real family, and I won't lie and say I'm sorry for wanting that as desperately as I do.

"Say you're sorry, and I'll let you suck my dick."

With a shit-eating grin, Jim leans down and places a kiss to one temple and then the other. All I can do is laugh, but he's crazy if he thinks I'm giving him an "I'm sorry" blow job.

"How about I let you fuck me in this field, and then we can discuss where we're putting the house," I say and reach up to take his cut off.

He laughs softly before his eyes heat. We undress one another in that field, exploring each other's bodies in ways we do every single time we make love. When we're naked and he's on his back, beneath me in the cold, damp grass, I let a single tear fall.

"I was so mad when you got this," I say with my eyes on the tattoo that takes up the whole of the outer side of his right forearm that says HERS in the same thick, black font that graces the Forsaken logo.

"That's because you're fucking crazy," he says. One hand works my clit, and the other pulls and twists one of my nipples. A chill runs up my spine that leaves me covered in gooseflesh.

"You make me fucking crazy." The words come out more as a moan than anything else.

"No, you came to me that way," he says dismissively. We continue like that for a few more minutes, with me admiring the tattoo he got for me and him prepping me for his dick. He found out the hard way that with his size I have to be well prepared first. Not that I'm complaining about the extra attention.

"I want one," I say, gliding my wet pussy over his hard cock. We shift and maneuver so he's at my entrance now. His quizzical expression tells me he doesn't understand. "I want one that matches. But only *after* my name is changed and I've adopted Ryan."

"Fuck yes." He slides inside me, hard and fast. And there's not another word between us aside from the occasional I-love-you as we make love in that cold, damp field that's soon to be our home.

CHAPTER EIGHTEEN

January 1999

My eyes are fixed on the red barn that sits in the middle of our property as Jim stomps his way down there, followed by a bunch of dogs. My man's shoulders heave in anger as he trudges through the mud, lifting his feet high in the air to keep from getting stuck in the soggy landscape. One of the puppies, Spartacus, keeps jumping up as they go, desperate for his dad's attention. But Jim ignores him, which is rare. He never fails to give Spartacus attention. I sigh in frustration and mentally kick myself for not dealing with the boys' mess before he got home.

Jim's not been the same since Sylvia passed just a few months ago. I haven't been the same either, though, and that's part of the problem. We've always been such a strong couple, able to withstand anything. Except this is different. Sylvia Stone did more for me and my boy than any other woman in my life. She took me under her wing and forced me to accept her as family. Not that it was all that hard to sway me, in retrospect.

"Dad's pissed." Ryan comes up and stands beside me. It's been just under two years since I met this kid, but he's already changed so much. Verging on eleven now, Ryan's just starting to go through puberty. I thought he was a handful as a nine-year-old, but I was wrong.

"Yeah, I wonder why," I say, nudging him with my shoulder. He just smirks. The little punk.

"Where's your brother?" I ask.

Ryan shrugs his shoulders and folds his arms over his chest, refusing to answer. His mood's suddenly turned sour, as it fucking should. All Jim asked was that the boys stop fucking around in the living room, and they couldn't even do that. If I'd taken the

Christmas tree down yesterday, like Jim "suggested," the boys wouldn't have knocked into it, and Sylvia's favorite ornament wouldn't have fallen to the floor and shattered in a hundred different pieces.

"Go find your brother," I say in a hard tone, but he doesn't move. Turning toward him, I do my best to check my temper.

"Ryan James, find your fucking brother and apologize."

Still, he doesn't move. And because I know my kid well enough to know that yelling at him doesn't do any good, I mimic his dad and stomp to the Christmas tree. I locate Sylvia's other favorite ornament and hold it by the string. Being so reckless with it makes me nervous, but Ryan needs to listen. When he turns around, his eyes are wide, and his lip trembles for a moment before he checks his nerves.

"You want me to break this one?" I ask.

Ryan shakes his head. "Stop!"

"You pushed your brother into the tree, and the ornament your grandma left him got broken. Seems to me that either you check your shit and apologize, or I break this one to even the fucking score."

"You wouldn't," Ryan says.

We stay in a standoff, me and this kid that's almost my height, arguing over shit we shouldn't be.

"How many years did you get with your grandma? Huh? How many?" He's silent. We've had this discussion before. My boys—all my boys—are grieving, each in their own ways, and none of them knows how to manage the pain. It's not like I have any better idea how to get out of bed in the morning, but somebody needs to keep this family together.

"Stop crying," Ryan says in something between a plea and a demand. I huff and try to will away the tears.

"Your brother never had a grandma until we came here. Sylvia left him that ornament because it represented this town—her home. She wanted Ian to know that this is his home, too. And now it's broken, and I can't put it back together. The absolute least you can do is say you're sorry to him."

"Okay," he says, and it's the closest thing to an agreement that I'm going to get. Ryan's never been good at expressing sorrow, and Sylvia is the first person he's ever really known who's died. He was too young to remember his mom, and Sylvia's cancer just came back so suddenly. We only had a few weeks before she was gone.

"And apologize to your father while you're at it. You might not get this right now, but he lost his mother, and he might not be crying over her, but mothers are important, and your dad's suffering just as much as you are."

Ryan's eyes are red and glassy now, but he doesn't want me to know that, so he looks away. Carefully, I set the ornament back on the tree and go give my boy a hug. I might be hearing things, but I swear the kid sniffles in my arms. When we're done, I send him off in search of Ian, and then I light a cigarette and take my ass outside.

Jim is on his way back from the barn now, and he's carrying a load of wood for the fireplace. His scowl tells me his mood is still too pissy for me to deal with, so I take a leisurely stroll to the mailbox and try to decompress.

An envelope, just a little bit too large for the box, sticks out. Ignoring the rest of the waiting mail, I grab the bubble mailer and inspect the label. There's no return address, but it was stamped in New York, and it's addressed to Ruby Buckley. My heart stops, my stomach does a flip, and I take one final drag from my cigarette before tossing it to the ground and stomping it out. I haven't received one of these since getting to Fort Bragg. Everything was so hectic after Ian and I left Texas that the packages stopped coming. They had nowhere to go. The last one I received was almost three years ago. The twins were only two then, and it was just a handful of pictures. Gloria, Mike's sister, risks a lot to send me these packages. Last year, when I finally got the word out to her that I was settled and didn't hear back, I just figured that was it. I wouldn't get anything else.

I open the envelope as quickly as possible while being careful not to damage anything inside. There's a video tape labeled "Christmas 1998," so it's really recent. A sob breaks free, and I clutch the tape to my chest. Everything I've gotten of my babies has been still photographs. I've never heard their voices or seen them move. Not since the day Mike took them.

Sucking in a deep breath and blowing it out slowly, I focus on calming myself down. There are also photos in the envelope—some candid and two professional ones from what looks to be their preschool—and a single sheet of white paper. Messy drawings in two different colors grace one side. I can barely breathe as I study the lines of the purple crayon and run my fingers over my baby girl's name in the bottom left corner. She wrote it herself, and her *r* is backward, but she's writing. Holy fuck, she's writing. Michael's side of the paper is more like three quarters of it, with his green crayon going right over his sister's purple. His name is even messier in his corner, but all his letters are facing the right way. My fingers trace his name as well, and I take care to note how hard he presses the crayon compared to his sister's soft lines. My babies are writing, and they're in preschool, and they're living this entire life without me.

"Babe," Jim shouts as he rushes up on me. Concern is clear in his voice, and so is the fact that he sprinted to me. He's out of breath and heaving when he gets to me. "What's wrong?"

I can't talk, so I just hand him their preschool photographs and nuzzle into Jim's flannel shirt in uncontrollable sobs. My eyes are closed as I strain for breath, but I can see their perfect faces so clearly in my head. Michael's all smiles with big brown eyes and little white teeth. He looks happy and confident, and even though he and Ian have very different features, I see his older brother in his eyes. Alexandra's smile is almost nonexistent in her school photo. She looks shy and demure. Like Esmeralda. I sob even harder at the thought. The last thing I want is for my daughter to grow up to be that timid. I want her to be strong and fearless.

Jim whistles as loud as he can and screams for the boys. I fight to pull myself together. By the time they appear from the neighboring woods, we're on the move and almost inside the house.

"This is a good thing, momma," Jim says. "Remember, we celebrate this shit." He smiles, full and genuine. I force myself to channel some of his mood and give the boys a soft smile when we get inside. Jim leads us into the living room where he takes the envelope from me and starts getting the tape ready.

"One of you get your mother some tissues. It's movie time."

CHAPTER NINETEEN

June 2005

"Very funny," I say, giving Ian the dirtiest look I can manage, which, admittedly, isn't very dirty right now. I'm laughing too hard to be actually annoyed with the situation. My entire front is covered in cold-ass water that smells like a bad mix of detergent and mold.

"I told you to turn off the water first," he says. My boy's a month shy of turning eighteen, and somehow we managed to get him to graduation. His brother dropped out last year, but that's okay, too.

Ryan's not an academic, and once he stopped going to school, I stopped having to drop everything to deal with the Fort Bragg PD for whatever violation my kid got himself slapped with that time. When he turned eighteen back in March, he started prospecting for the club anyway. That's his future. We've known it for years, and that's okay. But Ian, my high school graduate, is book savvy, and he should be the one fixing the washing machine right now.

"I told Ryan to do it," I say. It's a shit defense, and we both know it.

"Ry!" Ian shouts. To my surprise, Ryan actually appears from his bedroom after only being called once. This is a rarity. His jet-black hair is messed up, and he's got sleep in his eyes. It's two in the afternoon, but I choose to keep any comments about his life to myself. He's an adult, I remind myself, and as long as he takes care of what he's supposed to, I'm not going to interfere.

Well, I'm going to try not to interfere.

"Did you forget to do something?" I ask, trying to be kind about my tone. He's a pain in the ass fully awake and even worse when he's half-asleep. Ian's not buying it, though. He turns his light brown head of hair toward me, narrows his brown eyes, and gives me a look that speaks of a boy who's been putting up with his mom's excuses for his brother for far too long.

"Really?" he says in a monotone voice. I just shrug my shoulders and ignore him. I baby my boys, and if their dad were here, I'd baby him, too. I won't apologize for doting on the three of them. Ian's jaw ticks as he turns his attention back to his brother. "You forgot to turn off the water like Ma asked you to, you fucktard!"

"Hey! Not that you'd fucking understand, but I was out late on a run."

"Low blow, asshole," Ian snaps back. This has been a point of contention between my boys. Ryan is four months older, and since he dropped out of school, he was able to start prospecting right away. Ian doesn't turn eighteen for another month, so he's had to wait.

"Okay, stop it." A chill runs down my spine from the wet clothes sticking to my skin. "We have three more days before your dad comes home. It'd be a damn shame if one of you were missing when he gets released."

Jim's been serving the state at San Quentin for the last ten months. I can't wait for him to come home. I miss his touch and the sound of his voice when he first wakes up. I miss the sounds he makes when he's moving inside me and even the way he screams when he's mad. The boys miss him, too, even if they won't say it aloud. Ian especially. He refused to have any kind of graduation party until Jim could be here to celebrate with us. I actually cried tears of joys over that, knowing how much his dad's presence means to him. While Ian's been sullen, Ryan's been acting out. He's nearly ruined his friendship with Josh over his stupid antics.

The doorbell buzzes, surprising me. We don't often get people coming out here who think to ring a bell. I direct Ryan to get the door since it's his fucking fault that I'm half-drenched. He moves slowly and yawns upon opening the damn thing. What I see on the other side makes me freeze in place. A man, a little over six feet tall and with grayish-blond hair, stands in the doorway. He's got tattoos up and down his bare arms and up his neck. He even has a vine tattoo going up the side of his face to his temple. Over a black wife beater is a leather cut that declares him the vice president of the Mississippi Forsaken. I didn't need the cut to know who he is, though. I'd never be able to forget that vine tattoo or those piercing blue eyes that remind me so much of a young man I think of as my own.

"Can I help you?" Ryan asks in a tone that suggests he'd rather do anything but.

"No, but she can," he says, pointing an unsteady finger at me.

"You need to leave, Ghost. Now." I can't do this. Shit. Three fucking days until Jim's released, and Ghost shows up now. I knew he'd been released, but this situation is entirely too fucked for words. Not only do my boys not know anything about Ghost, but the fucking man shows up at my house half out of his mind. His eyes are bloodshot and unfocused. He snarls as he speaks and isn't entirely steady on his feet.

"Not without what I came for," he says and steps into the house.

Ryan lifts a hand to the man's chest and gives him a push outside. Despite Ghost's inebriated state, he barely budges and rebounds quickly. He's in Ryan's face and pushing him backward. Ryan stumbles, barefoot, and catches himself but only just before hitting the floor with his ass. Ian lunges forward, shoving Ghost toward the door. The boys restrain him long enough for me to breathe. Memories that have never ceased to haunt me rise to the surface.

Frantically looking around for something, anything, to help, I find my hands shaking. I hate this man and what he's done. It's bad enough that he fathered one child against the mother's will, but then he came back to town and did it again with one of the lost girls. I won't ever forget Rage telling me that story. I never thought much of it before, but it makes sense now why Josh has always been so close with the club while his mom tries to stay so distant. I just figured the boys were friends and she tolerated Forsaken for her kid. But that's not the case at all.

Quickly, I grab the first thing that can be used as a weapon—the wrench I was using on the washer—and use it to guard myself. I know what Ghost wants, and he's not getting it. The lost girl he raped pressed charges, and he went away for it. I know where she is because I keep an eye on her. Despite who her father is, Jenny is a beautiful girl. She has a good life with her mom and stepdad. I won't give Ghost that information even if he tries to kill me for it. Some things are worth losing for. It's just a shame that Josh won't ever meet his sister.

"Ma," Ian shouts. Ghost is bitching and cursing at the boys to let him go, but they're not listening.

Because they're smart and know a psychopath when they see one. "Who the fuck is this guy?"

"I'm Josh Wilcox's father," Ghost yells. His eyes are wild, and he takes a deep breath, shoving Ryan against the wall beside them. Ian tries to restrain him, but he can't. Without giving it another thought, I lunge forward and swing the wrench out, making contact with Ghost's torso.

Ryan's shouting, Ian's trying to avoid the swing of the wrench, and Ghost is gasping for breath as he doubles over and crumples to the floor. The three of us step back, and we stare at the man on the floor.

"Duke's dad?" Ryan asks, his eyebrows raised. He uses the nickname the club only recently gave to Josh. "When the fuck were you gonna tell me, or maybe Duke, that you know his fucking dad?"

Even Ian is giving me a judgmental glare.

"This piece of shit isn't his dad—he's his mother's rapist," I say. I'm seething, my chest heaves, and despite the seriousness of the situation, I'm more angry than scared. I don't know how Ghost still has his cut, but he does. He's the fucking vice president of a charter that's not known for playing well with others. They'd challenge us over this, even if this asshole ends up walking away from it.

"I'm calling Butch." I back away from the situation and set the wrench down on the entertainment center, trusting the boys to watch Ghost while I find my mobile. It's on the bathroom sink, so I grab it and rush into my bedroom and snag the nearest hand gun at my disposal. Everything is quiet, for the most part, in the living room, so I take a moment to call Butch from my room. All I have to say is Ghost's name and he tells me he's on his way and hangs up the phone.

I've barely hung up and shoved the phone in my pocket when a loud crash sounds from the other room. Ryan's screaming at Ian, and Ian's screaming at Ghost. When I rush in, I find Ghost has Ryan pinned up against the wall. The entertainment center is wrecked, with it only half standing. The other half is a busted flat screen TV and crushed sound system. My stomach drops. Jim had Grady get that ridiculously expensive thing in honor of Ryan's prospecting and Ian's graduation. The angle Ghost has Ryan at is making it difficult for Ian to help. My boy is turning blue, though. I need to do something before he really gets hurt. Raising the gun to shoot, I'm blocked by Ian stepping in my way. His back is to me as he manages to free Ryan from Ghost's grasp using sheer force of will. Ghost slides down the half-broken entertainment center and grabs the wrench. He swings it high and hits Ian right in his chest. I watch in horror as my boy falls backward and sucks in a shallow breath on his way. His eyes fall closed as he hits the floor.

Ryan rushes at Ghost, narrowly dodging the wrench he swings. I've shot a gun many times—Jim's seen to that. I've even shot a man before. I've just never taken a life. But as I raise the gun again, I have no fear or trepidation about pulling the trigger. This man is a rapist and an abuser. He's everything I hate, and I want his reign of terror to end. For once and for all. Flipping off the safety, I get Ghost in my line of sight and take a deep breath. Before I can pull the trigger, Ian's strong arms wrap around me. His firm hand squeezes mine on the gun, forcing me to release it, and then he spins me around, shielding me from what's about to happen. Without a moment to waste, Ian releases me and shoves me backward. I scramble forward just as Ian pushes Ryan to the side and places the barrel of the gun to Ghost's temple. I watch in horror as he pulls the trigger, painting the wall with dripping blood.

I've never taken a life before. The only time I came close was when that piece of shit violated my boy when he was a kid. Even then, I maimed him and left him for the cops to deal with. I couldn't bring myself to do it. And now, I'm watching a man's blood drip down the wall in my living room after my seventeen-year-old son shot him in the head.

Ryan bends over and starts dry heaving. He's breathing heavy, and his hands are shaking as he tries to keep himself upright with his hands on his knees. I take a step toward Ian, who's lowered the gun, put the safety back on, and placed it in the waistband of his jeans, but I stop. He's totally calm but silent, and that worries me. I redirect my attention to Ryan and move to comfort him, but I can't. I look back at Ian to find him pulling the bayonet knife he carries from its holder at his waist and grabbing Ghost by the throat. His body is limp, the effects of death slowly settling in. Ian's brown eyes stare into Ghost's dead blues blankly as he scrawls the word *sin* into the dead man's forehead.

Right as he finishes, Butch rushes through the open front door and stops. I turn to look at my longtime friend with tears in my eyes. And I just stand there, frozen, unsure what to do. One of my boys is freaking out because his brother just killed a man. And the other is resurrecting old trauma by carving up a man's flesh. My heart breaks in a million pieces for the little boy who found out all too soon how awful the world could be and the young man who now stands before me, eyeing a dead body with a sick aura of peace about him.

I can't help but feel responsible for this. My life choices have made my boy a killer.

CHAPTER TWENTY

May 2014

Jim's hands travel down my bare sides, caressing every inch he can get his lotion-covered hands on. He licks his lips lasciviously as I slowly part my knees before putting them back together. I could open up for him, but then the massage would be over, and I'm not ready for that. It's not all that often that my man spoils me like this. I can get an orgasm whenever and however I want—that he's always game for. It's the drawn out foreplay that he has to be prodded to initiate. So I'm going to milk this time for all it's worth. Rubbing my thighs together, I moan softly and clench them together despite Jim's insistent attempt to gently pry them apart.

"You being a tease, momma?"

"I like being chased," I say in defense and wave a finger at the nearby lotion bottle. Jim gives me a flat look and squirts some more lotion into his palm, then continues with the rubdown.

"Been chasing you for twenty years," he says, his hands dipping around the back of my thighs and pulling me forward. A laugh turns to a smile as he manages to part my thighs.

"And you'll chase me for twenty more," I say confidently. If there's one thing in this world I don't doubt, it's this man's love for me. And I never want him to doubt my love for him. So while he's massaging my inner thighs, and it feels incredible, I need to show him that the feeling is mutual. Not that I think he doubts my feelings. After two decades together and nearly that many married, we're solid.

"But then I'm done," he says as he watches me pull myself into a sitting position. I squirt some lotion into the palm of my hands, rub them together, and then proceed to massage Jim's thighs.

"Done, huh? Just like that?" We're face-to-face

now, so close that I can practically taste the coffee on his breath. He smiles and leans in, giving me a sweet kiss to my lips. We're both smiling when he pulls away. For the millionth time since we became us, I've wished that I could have given him a baby. I made a vow to myself, though, that I wouldn't have another kid after the twins. Jim's always respected that. Even though there was that one surprise, when it ended seven weeks in, we were sad, but we moved on. It wasn't meant to be for us, and that's okay. We have our boys, and I'm perfectly fulfilled with that, but I know Jim's always secretly yearned for a kid that carries both our genes.

"In another twenty, I'm gonna be too old to chase you, woman."

"I call bullshit," I say, leaning in and nibbling his lip. We fall into each other, laughing and kissing the whole way. Lazy afternoons making love to my husband don't happen near as often as I'd like, so I make sure to treasure every moment I have like this.

My mobile sounds from the bedside table with a tone I thought I'd never hear. It's a high-pitched squealing sound that I can't ignore. Jim stills, the joy in his eyes disappearing immediately. It's Gloria's ring tone. We scramble to grab it before it stops ringing. Both of us with shaking hands and fear in our hearts.

Gloria.

There's only one reason Gloria would call, and it sends an anchor to the pit of my stomach. When I answer the phone, my voice shakes.

"They're safe, for now," she says in a panicked voice. Her New York accent is thicker than I remember, her voice huskier, and I know it's because she never did give up smoking. I probably sound the same to her. "But Alex is in hot water. You need to get her out of here. Now."

I turn my eyes to Jim who's head is butted up to the phone. He pulls back and gives me a confident nod and the most pathetic excuse for a smile I've ever seen. Taking the phone from me, he sets the wheels of our trip in motion.

I have no idea what awaits me. I just know that I'm going to meet my daughter. After almost twenty years apart, I'm going to see my baby girl. The devastation that overtakes me is something I can't explain to Jim. Even after he gets off the phone with Gloria, I'm at a loss for words. I should be happy, he says. Scared and worried, yes. But happy. I don't feel happy, though. I feel like I'm being taunted with much-needed oxygen that's going to be taken away just as I'm suffocating. Like I shouldn't hope that this is really happening. That despite the circumstances, this won't end well and she won't live up to the hundred different things I expect her to be. Or that she's going to hate me. Or even worse, that she'll never know who I am or how much I've grieved not having her in my life.

Jim stands from the bed and starts to dress in a hurry. I stare at him in part confusion and part anger. Where the hell is he going? As if he can read my mind, he crosses the room, grabs me behind my neck and pulls me in.

"I'm cashing in that marker. We're going to get our girl."

CHAPTER TWENTY-ONE

Jim
Brooklyn, New York
April 2016
Mancuso's downfall

Slowly, I pry my eyes open only to be met with the harsh, bright lights of the hospital. It takes me a moment to realize what's going on and where I am. A low-level buzz rings in my ears, worrying me. I don't know a whole ton about medical stuff, but I know a ringing in your ears is usually not a good thing. Fuck. Instead of torturing myself with the unwelcome noise and fucking interrogation lights, I let my eyes fall closed while I hope for it all to just go away. A few minutes pass, at least it feels like a few minutes, before the ringing stops. When it does, I realize that it wasn't in my ears at all, but rather a nearby machine. I hate hospitals more than anything.

"Mr. Stone?" A soft, feminine voice calls out to me, forcing me to push myself back into the world. I'd rather stay like this, stock still and in silence with my eyes closed. But if this nurse can do something about the lights, I'm going to play ball.

"Yeah," I grunt. My throat is sore and uncomfortably gravelly. Forcing one eye open, I size up the intruder. She's got to be close to six feet tall, and she's got broad shoulders, with honey-blonde hair and gray-blue eyes. She's pretty, even in her animal-print scrubs, and she's giving me a kind smile. Well then.

"It's nice to see you awake," she says. I nod my head, not really wanting to repeat the whole talking thing again.

"I'm Vicky, your nurse for about the next thirty minutes. I'll be sure to bring your new nurse around before I leave so you don't feel too abandoned." With that, she moves around the small space, checking machines and writing things down on her clipboard.

For the first time since I woke up, I really survey the space around me. I'm not exactly in a room, so I think I'm still in emergency. There's a wall to my left, but to my right and in front of me are glass walls that are mostly shielded by a bright and colorful curtain. My view of the nurse's station is partially blocked by a man's broad, suit-clad shoulder and his short black hair. Craning my neck around, I see a mural on the wall behind me that's made up of teddy bears, balloons, and bumble bees.

"We had to put you in the peds corner," the nurse says with a head nod toward the glass door across the room. The man is still there. Realizing I still don't understand, Vicky leans in and checks my vitals. In a hushed tone, she says, "Detective Davis insisted you be in a secure room. It doesn't matter how many times your wife has told him how you and your stepdaughter were injured, the detective doesn't seem to believe her. He's been standing guard for hours now."

"I don't need his protection," I say. Davis. That name sounds familiar, but my brain is foggy. On the other side of the glass door, the suited man I now know as Detective Davis shifts in place. His hands gesture to something across the emergency room from us, and then he pulls out his phone, puts it to his ear, and walks away.

"I don't think that's why he's here," Vicky says.

"Alex, shit," I say, finally realizing I haven't asked about our girl. She has to be okay, not fine, but okay. "I need you to check on Alexandra Mancuso's condition for me."

"I've been keeping tabs on Ms. Mancuso off and on since you guys came in. She's stable. Despite the depth of the cuts on her face, she lost minimal blood. The skin will take time to heal, and it will scar over, but she's lucky."

"She's lucky? That girl is anything but lucky, lady."

"That was a poor choice of words. I'm sorry." Vicky sounds like she has more to say, but the whooshing sound from the opening of the glass door distracts me from listening. A tired smile overtakes my face at the sight before me.

"There's my man," Ruby says as she pushes her way through the door. Her lips are turned up at the corners, but I wouldn't call it a smile because it doesn't reach her eyes. She's wearing the same blood-stained clothes like a shield. I know my woman. If she changes and has to wash the blood off, it makes this all real, and then she has to deal with it.

With a few steps, she's hovering over me awkwardly. Tentatively, I reach up and grab the back of her neck and pull her lips to mine. My shoulder is stiff, and I'm weak, but I do my best to keep from showing it. I give my toes a wiggle and move my legs as much as I can bring myself to. My arms are lethargic, as is the rest of me, but they don't hurt exactly. When I deepen the kiss and pull my woman in closer, my abdomen aches from the strain of it. We keep on like this, just indulging in each other. When we finally pull away, I notice Vicky in the corner, her cheeks bright red and her nose shoved in her clipboard. Ruby sucks in a ragged breath and licks her lips as she stares at me through hooded eyes. My dick is at half-mast, as is evident through the thin, aging bed linens. Vicky does her best not to notice, but I catch her looking anyway and give her a wink.

Just as I'm having fun with the pretty nurse, my mobile phone buzzes from somewhere near my head. I try to reach for it, but Ruby slaps me away, saying, "You're going to pop your stitches." She stares at the notification screen. "Text from Duke," she says before handing the phone over.

Twenty years ago I knew she'd be the perfect old

lady. Didn't take the club long to catch on. The day after I brought my girl home, I asked the club to vote her in. Eighteen months later, after we'd already been married for almost six months, Rage inked her with the Forsaken warrior. Part of the warrior's blade peeks out from under her leather jacket on her collar bone. Twenty years and she still looks at me with the same amount of love and trust she did the day I made her mine.

"Will you check that text message?" she chides playfully. "It might be important. Once we're back home, we'll have forever to stare at each other like lovesick teenagers."

"Still won't be enough time," I say with my eyes on my phone. Pulling up Duke's text, I stare in horror at the image that comes through. Duke's face is bloody and bruised, with cuts over and under his left eye. His nose is clearly broken, and dried blood is coming out of his nostrils. His right eye is swollen. There's an anger in his expression that matches the hate I feel in my heart right now. What the fuck is going on now? Another text arrives, this one reading, TAKE OUR KING, WE TAKE YOUR DUKE. SWAP. 6A. PLACE TBA.

"Fuck," I say a little louder than intended and quickly forward the messages to Wyatt. I'm guessing whoever in Mancuso's organization had the nerve to take one of our guys doesn't have any more inside intel, because shit like this gets directed at the top. I'm not at the top anymore.

Vicky the Nurse pulls her attention from the computer screen she's staring at, in shock.

"Sorry. My son just texted me. I've been asking him to come see me, but he's in the other room with my stepdaughter. He, uh, won't leave her side."

Vicky looks through the glass door, her eyebrows raised in surprise. Ruby leans over me, seeing something I can't, and clears her throat as she focuses her attention on the nurse. "They only met two years ago. They weren't raised together."

"Uh-huh," Vicky says, mouth agape.

"We're not like that, I swear," Ruby says with a disturbed look on her face. Vicky blinks and then turns toward Ruby, who says, "Hey, uh, nurse, do you think it'd be okay to bring our daughter in here to see her dad?"

The nurse turns back to the door, bites her lip, and scrunches her face. I groan at the thought of what she's seeing. We really need to find a better way to explain our family to people so they don't look at us like we're a fucking freak-show. Once Vicky composes herself, she says she doesn't think that will be a problem and then excuses herself. She also promises to keep Detective Davis away from my room for as long as she can.

When she's gone, Ruby tells me how Ryan was lying in bed with Alex, groping one of her boobs with his mouth at her neck. She swatted him away, at least, but otherwise, it was a straight-up PG-13 scene going on in there.

I try to laugh at the situation, but all I can think about is that fucking picture. I keep my phone down but in my hand, so just in case something else comes through, my woman can't see it.

A few minutes pass before Ian and Mindy file into the room, followed by Michael. Eventually, Ryan backs into the room, pulling Alex in a wheelchair right along with him. I get them all settled and check in with Alex, who just nods her head in response. Ruby and Ryan explain that it's painful for her to move her facial muscles, especially since she's trying to take as little pain medicine as possible.

"Makes her too drowsy, and fuck if I'm letting Cub lay up in here, defenseless," Ryan says. He rubs her shoulders. Our girl looks damn miserable. She tries to communicate with me, but the bandages on her face make it difficult.

"Don't, sweetheart," I say when she tries to talk. "I'm okay. We're going to be okay." I don't tell her that we're going to be okay because her father will soon be dead. Instead, I just try to give our girl a little comfort when I can. She's had enough devastation. We all have. When we get home, I'm going to take it easy. I'll be retired, spending my days drinking whiskey on my porch and sinking into my old lady. Life's going to be good. It'll be easy.

But before it can be easy, it's going to be hard.

With a sigh, I toss my phone to Ian. Ryan's likely to break the fucking thing first. It takes him less than thirty seconds to look at the picture and accompanying message and to start relaying its contents to the room. While he's got the phone in hand, he sends the message around to the guy's burners and then hands it to Michael. As predicted, when Ryan sees the photo of his best friend, all bloodied and bruised, he gets mad enough that he kicks at the nearest wall. Thankfully, it wasn't one of the glass ones.

"They're dead," Ryan snaps. "They're fucking dead." Ryan's outrage is only matched by his mother's, who spits out roughly the same thing. I give her hand a squeeze to try to calm her down. Nobody rages like a momma bear.

"No doubt, son," I say, "But you want to keep it down so Detective Davis doesn't try arresting your ass before we can get our boy back?"

Alex's eyes dart up to Ryan. She pulls down on his cut and signals for his phone. Doing a quick about-face, he crouches down in front of her and tries to decipher her request. I don't interject, rather, I lie in silence and watch. My son, who is all temper and impulse and until a few years ago only ever cared about himself, is quietly trying to understand his girlfriend's needs. When she grows tired of playing charades with him, she reaches into his cut and pulls the phone out herself. Ryan's eyes soften and crinkle in the corners as a smile overtakes his face. She types something out that's just for him, judging by the light that shines in his eyes, but then types something else right after. Ryan places a kiss to the top of her head and stands to his full height.

"Cub says Davis is the pig who double-crossed her."

"Wait," Michael says. He's been fairly quiet in the corner so far, his eyes working a strategy. "Adam

Davis? The prick who arrested me?"

"The very same," Ian says. He places a hand on Mindy's shoulder and gives it a squeeze. "If Scavo wants his sister safe, he better get her out of that house and fast. Her husband, the good officer, has been promoted to detective, and he's been working closely with the FBI. Way I see it, there's only one reason Davis is here."

"Shit. So that's his angle. After two years, he's still trying to press RICO." Michael pulls his phone out and shoots off a quick message, then shoves it back in his pocket.

"Not only that, but if the feds can prove a connection between Forsaken and Mancuso, and they use RICO, and we're all done for," Ian says. Then he does something with his phone and nods his head at Michael.

"Well, that's not going to happen," Michael says. He pulls his phone out and messes with the screen. Then he curses. "Fucking Tony. You know this is him, right?" His attention is on Alex now. She nods her head. When she came to us two years ago, she was all tears and soft edges all the time. She's toughened up a lot since the last time we were in New York. She still loves her father and cousin, I know that. But she doesn't seem sad about their fate anymore.

"I think I know where they got Duke," Michael says, studying his phone. "There's a big-ass ventilator in Fortino's old warehouse—the one the feds seized. The thing weighs a fucking ton. And it looks just like the thing behind your boy's head."

"How sure are you about this?" Ryan sizes Michael up, and possibly for the first time, he doesn't look like he hates his stepbrother. Progress, however small, is fucking needed.

"I'd bet my life on it," Michael says.

"Then we better get going." Ryan straightens his back, puffs his chest out, and checks his waistband for his trusty knife. When he bends at the waist and reaches to his ankle, I know he's checking for the .22 he carries there.

"Wait for your president, son," I say in warning. "Going off half-cocked is going to get you hurt—or worse."

"They have my brother," Ryan says. Ian's eyes bore into the side of Ryan's head, essentially begging him to look his way. When he finally does, Ryan shakes his head in response. "What? Suddenly

Duke's not your boy?"

"Don't." Ian's tone is ice cold. "You of all people know not to question my loyalty. Especially for Duke."

"Shit." Michael's head is tilted toward the glass. He's got the curtain pulled back, surveying the rest of the emergency room. "Feds are coming. We better break this up."

Everybody moves into action, with Michael and Ian heading out to contact the rest of the club. Ruby gives me a wry smile as she grabs Mindy's arm and drags her from my room. I barely hear her mutter, "Trust me," on their way out. Within moments, Ruby's screaming at the top of her lungs about Mindy trying to fuck her husband.

My eyes widen in response as do Alex's. We stare at each other in shock before a smile lights up her face. She winces in pain and sighs unhappily. Her hand finds its way to the bandages on her face. Nurse Vicky shows up a moment later and escorts Alex back to her room. Ryan's eyes follow the retreating duo, but he doesn't follow.

"I know what you want to do, but don't you even think about it."

"I'm not leaving him there. We wait until six and they'll ambush us. We won't have to worry about RICO and the bitch-ass feds because we'll be dead."

"I'm not saying six. I'm saying you take it to Pres. You rush in alone and you will end up dead. They want Mancuso. He's the only way you walk out of there alive *and* with our boy."

Ryan bounces, antsy on his feet, unable to stay still. His eyes dart around the room. He sucks in a shaky breath and throws his arms in the air. One step back toward the door and then another.

"Son, don't." My words do no good. Ryan rushes out of the room and disappears around the corner. I grab at my abandoned phone on my bed next to me and call Ian. He doesn't answer. Neither does Michael or any of my brothers. Fuck. *Think, Jim, think.* I focus on finding a solution to solving the problem my son's about to create, but I can't.

Except one.

"Okay, legs. Don't fail me now," I say to myself as I move to sit up. It's painful at best, but not so blinding that I can't keep moving. Once I'm sitting up all the way, I slowly pull the IV out of my arm and detach everything else that's keeping me bedridden.

Ruby's and Mindy's screams are barely audible now, their voices trailing down the crowded space. Christ, I hope they don't get themselves arrested. A shrill alarm sounds, followed by a clicking noise and the sprinklers going off. Everything gets coated in cold water, including the floor. I'm no pussy, but even I'm nervous about sliding around on the wet linoleum. I don't let it deter me, though. I slide off the bed, despite the slight wobble of my legs, and walk out of the room as inconspicuously as possible. Which isn't fucking easy considering my bare ass is on display for all to see. When we get home, I'm going to kill my son for making me do this. A man gets stabbed, he should be able to recover in fucking peace.

CHAPTER TWENTY-TWO

Ruby

My crazy-ass daughter-in-law turns toward me and sneers. She lunges forward, but the cuffs on her wrists make tackling me improbable. Detective Davis stands behind her, one hand wrapped around her upper arm.

"Settle down, ladies."

I roll my shoulders and try to ignore the pinching of the metal on my wrists. Davis eyes me questioningly, like he doesn't believe that we're genuinely pissed at each other. He's been giving us these looks since before they slapped the cuffs on us. I don't pay him much attention, though. I'd rather he be out here with us than inside with my guys. I guess in a strange way I should be grateful to the sorry fuck. If it weren't for Davis trying to score points with the feds, I never would have gotten the chance to meet Alex and Michael. They would have forever lived in my heart as a pair of crying infants who Mike took from me. But now? Thanks to this eager beaver, I have *all* of my kids in my life.

Something feels off. Maybe it's just because it's the middle of the night and I'm a firm believer that good things don't happen at three a.m. It just feels like there's something horribly wrong, and I can't put my finger on it. Mindy and I were supposed to be the distraction, but then somebody pulled the fire alarm just as we were almost out of the emergency room door. That was when the feds starting grilling us about Jim's and Alex's injuries and, of course, the fire alarm. We knew nothing about that last thing, though, which is what was particularly curious for Detective Davis. I'm just hoping he isn't always this hungry for a case and is having an off day. Either way, we need to get out of New York and fast. We didn't come this far only to lose half our family to general lockup because this asshole wants to make it big in his department.

"Okay, boys, fun's over," a woman says as she quickly approaches from around the corner of the building. When she comes into view, the first thing I see is her striking red hair. She's average in every other way, despite the expensive ass skirt and blazer she's wearing. In one hand, she carries a leather briefcase, and in the other, a coffee. Her eyes lock with mine. "I'm Kimberly George with Harrison and Hart. I represent the Forsaken Motorcycle Club. Unless you're planning on arresting either or both of these women, please remove the handcuffs immediately."

Davis guffaws, stumbling all over himself while the agents gripe but do as Ms. George says. I don't know where she came from or who called her, but I'm damn grateful they did. Within minutes, the officers and the feds find their way off hospital property, and Mindy and I are left with our mysterious attorney. A quick conversation about how Gloria hired her on our behalf ensues, and then we go our separate ways. My phone's buzzed in my pocket no less than half a dozen times already. By the time I get to Jim's messages, Mindy's already on the phone with Ian. She snaps her fingers at me and points to the parking garage, then takes off running. I have no choice but to follow.

She stops, finally, and turns to me. In less than a minute, she lays it all out for me. Including the part where Jim followed Ryan out of the hospital in a mad dash. Horrified, I check my phone again. This time, I listen to Jim's voice messages. They're not much more than five or six words each, all spoken in code, confirming exactly what Mindy's just told me. At this point, I'm going through the motions, trying not to think about it. Not about the implications of being handcuffed and questioned by not only the police but the feds as well. Not about the fact that my husband, who's just barely started to recover from a gnarly stab wound, is off chasing my son down before he gets himself killed.

And I'm definitely not thinking about the ashen look on Ian's face as he pulls the van up and Michael and Alex open the back for us to hop in. Or the way my boy speeds like a maniac through the streets of Brooklyn even though we all know local law enforcement has it out for us. I don't even respond when Mindy tries to ask me if I'm okay. I just can't bring myself to do or say anything.

My hands grip the bench beneath me as we take each turn faster and faster than the last. Ian isn't one to be rattled. He's my steady one. And yet here he is, freaking out. A heaviness settles over me as I prepare myself for the worst. I guess I didn't let myself feel it earlier. I just kind of told myself that we would come out here, take care of business, and then head home. I thought it'd be easy—well, easier—and that would be it. We'd be done. I'd never have to see Brooklyn again, and my worst memories would still be from the day I lost my twins. But that's not my life. My life is content for a warning label about poor choices.

The familiar rumble of motorcycles—not just a few, but many—grows behind us. I tense up, looking around frantically at my surroundings. It's the guys. Because of course it is. I don't know why I started panicking.

"Mom," Alex says quietly from beside me. "Are you okay?" Her brown eyes are filled with worry and a sadness that I wish I could replace with something less daunting. Behind her, Michael's expression is near identical.

"I'm worried about Ryan," I admit. Ever since I met the boy, he's been going off and doing stupid shit like this. But it was different when the stakes weren't so high. He's no longer getting into fights on the playground and ditching class or even antagonizing the Fort Bragg PD. This time, he's trying to take on what's left of the detractors of the

Mancuso crime family. I of all people know that those people don't fuck around.

"We're a block out," Ian shouts from the driver's seat. Blinking away my climbing fear, I move into action and put on my bulletproof vest as does everybody else. Somehow Ian manages to get his on without losing control of the van.

"Jim doesn't have a weapon," I say immediately upon the realization that he left empty-handed. I don't even know if he had shoes or pants even. The last time I saw him, he was in a hospital gown, all hooked up to machines in bed. Maybe I'm slow to the issue, because nobody says anything for a long while. I'm worried about Jim's stitches more than anything, but my man is smart. He's not the one I fear for.

"A couple of the guns were missing when we got to the van," Michael says reassuringly. "Bet Pop grabbed 'em before hot-wiring his ride."

For the briefest of moments, Ian's eyes meet mine in the rearview mirror. He knows more than he's telling, but we don't have time for me to grill him, so I let him keep his secrets. Usually when Ian doesn't want to tell me something it's because either his father or brother are off doing something I'll disapprove of. In this case, he's right to be tight-lipped. If I had my way, Jim would be laid up in that damn hospital bed still.

Ian turns the corner off the street and down the empty road toward the entrance to the docks. We all have our guns in hand and safeties off. Mindy's in position to open the doors when Ian stops. We went over this, so I refuse to be nervous. My family is to descend on theirs, never taking our eyes off them. Since we know basically nothing about where we are or what's about to go down, that's the extent of our grand rescue plan. We've worked with less in the past, and that was with fewer people. It's not much, but it's something to keep me steady.

"Get ready." Ian's hard voice carries through the van. He starts to say something about how we women are backup and not front line, but the deafening sound of a gun blast masks his words. We all jump, terrified but at the ready. When Ian brings the van to a stop, Mindy flings the doors open, and we all pour out almost at once. My hands shake as I survey the scene before me. No more than fifteen feet from the entrance, I stand struck with horror.

The warehouse has a large pull-down steel door that's rolled up right now, exposing the interior to the outside. I creep up toward it, my family at my sides.

The bikes come to a screeching halt around me, and before I know it, Wyatt's blocking my view, telling me to stand down. I don't listen, though, because he husband and my son are in there. Voices scream at us, some in English and others in Italian. I back off Wyatt and take it in. There can't be more than ten or eleven of Mancuso's men in the room. They're standing in a line, facing us, guns out. In the center, in front of them, is Duke, bound and gagged to a metal folding chair. But that's not what sends a chill down my spine. It's the sight of a man with a gun to Ryan's head. Jim stands behind the man, a pistol in hand, pointing it at the guy's head.

We get closer, telling Mancuso's men to stand down. Not surprisingly, they don't. Negotiations continue, with Michael taking lead. The man with the gun on Ryan won't listen to reason, citing his loyalty to Carlo. I fall back, behind Michael this time, not knowing what to do, but trusting in the club to make it better. Nobody is standing down. But then the man with the gun on Ryan sets it all in motion. He cocks his gun, the barrel pressed into my son's head.

"No!" Jim shouts. He fires off a shot, hitting the man between his shoulder blades. Jim's wearing a pair of blue hospital scrubs with no shoes, and he stand uneasily on his bare feet. The thrust of the shot knocks the wind out of him, and he fights to suck in air. The man in front of him stumbles backward into my husband, and they both sink to the ground in a hard crash. My feet take off for my man, but Michael pulls me back, holding me in his suit-clad arms.

"Let me go," I plea. A guttural scream emanates from my lungs as I kick at my youngest son. I should stop fighting, but I can't stop myself. I should do a lot of things, and all I can do is scream and cry.

"We got this. It's okay," Michael says.

When I finally calm down enough to see what's happening around us, I suck in a deep breath and watch as all the pieces fall into place. Our senior ranking club members have Mancuso's men dropping their weapons and going back to their single file line. Torque frees Duke from his restraints. The prospects and old ladies are keeping watch on the warehouse's entrances and exits. A veritable wall of people now separates Jim from the Italians. Ryan's moved into action and pulls the man who attacked Jim off of him. In his right hand, he holds a small knife. It and his hand are both covered in blood. And in this moment I know. It's not his, but Jim's.

My man lays motionless on the concrete floor.

Ryan hovers over him, holding his head up with one hand and trying to make him more comfortable with the other. With the Italians under control, Ian puts his gun away and crouches beside his father. It's all so surreal. Mindy, Alex, and Holly stand with their backs to Jim as directed by Grady. I've seen this before. This is similar to what they did when Chief was shot.

But Chief died.

As if finally catching on that this is really happening, my body responds to my desperate need to be with my man. I shove my way past Diesel and Elle, who stand in front of Jim, trying to tell me that I don't want to see him like this. But of course I do. I drop to the pavement and pull him into my arms just like I did the night before. I don't even look for the wound this time. Ryan's already got something to soak up the leaking blood and keep pressure on it. That bastard hit him in a near identical place to where Mike stabbed him last night. Fuck.

"Don't worry, momma," Jim says, his words slow and slurred. "He just grazed me."

"I know, baby." I won't fight with him in this moment even though I can see that it's anything but just a graze.

Ian's eyes lift to mine. He has pretty much mastered Jim's look of disapproval by now. There's a sadness twinged in there, too. Maybe it's just me and it's not as bad as I think it is. Maybe I'm just crazy.

"Two knife wounds," Ian says, clearing his voice. "Motherfucker had aim. Got Pop right in the stitches."

"It only just sounds bad," Jim says. Liar. Even I know what's happening here. I place a hand on his forehead. It's so hot, way too hot to be normal. He's also sweating profusely, and his hand shakes violently as he tries to raise it up enough to demonstrate how little the issue really is. He's pale with purple circles around his eyes, and every single breath is more difficult than the last.

"Quit lying to us, Dad." Ryan holds Jim's other hand in his. His knuckles are white from the effort to keep from snapping. "It's bad, and we all know it."

Jim gives our boys a sad smile and nods his head. For my part, I hold Jim's torso tight to my chest and kiss the top of his head.

"In that case," Jim says softly, "Give her what she wants. You won't ever regret it making her happy. With your girls or mine, just make them happy.

"No doubt. You two are my greatest creations." Jim sucks in a ragged breath and looks at Ryan first and then Ian. There are unshed tears in his eyes that slay me. I'm so numb, I don't think I'm feeling it. I'm just forcing myself to act like I'm here, in the moment. In reality, my brain's already shut down.

I know what this is—this is death.

"I love you, momma." His words come out on a gasp as his eyes dart side to side involuntarily. His body is shutting down.

"Why couldn't you have just stayed in your hospital bed?" The rawness in my voice sounds foreign to my own ears. The volume shocks me. It's as if part of me is here, screaming at Jim about what he should have done. Even though I know him staying put would have gotten our boy killed. A crushing guilt overcomes me. I won't price my husband's life over my any of my sons'. I hate that shit so much, so I push it down as far as I can and hope it never resurfaces.

"Told you I'd walk through fire for you," he says. The last few words are mumbled, barely audible, and they end on the last gasp of air that leaves my husband's body.

And he's gone.

We don't move for a long while, just stay like that, without a single word to pass between us. Ryan moves first, removing the piece of torn shirt from Jim's side. He looks up at the human shield the girls have created. My eyes follow his. Alex's body shakes in silent sobs from what she's just witnessed. Her face is contorted in ways that must be painful for her and her scars, but she cries anyway. Still, no sound escapes her. Immediately, Ryan pulls her down to him, and he lets out a cry that is so honest, I know I'll never forget it.

Mindy moves in to comfort Ian, but he pushes her off and stomps away. Once he's standing over the body of the man who took his father from him, he gives it a kick. And then another and another. He doesn't let up until Grady drags him away. It's only then that my boy's eyes dart up, and he looks for Mindy. When he finds her, the tears fall openly from his eyes.

There's no shame in crying, I used to tell him.

Even the strongest of men cry.

Looking down at the man in my arms, all limp and lifeless and still so formidable—even in death—I work to pull his deadweight up higher, so I can hug him better. It's not easy, but I make it happen. Everybody is sort of immobile now, some intently watching me, others determined to do anything but. I ignore them and give myself this final moment with my man. It starts with one tear, and then there's many. A memory surfaces, and it knocks me on my ass.

You don't shut us out, he'd once told me. I was depressed over the twins' birthday and had pretty much given up on the entire world. My pushy, determined, loving man told me I don't get to quit when our kids need us.

"They need me now," I whisper to myself on repeat until I can bring myself to do what I need to. With one final moment, I brush Jim's hair back from his face and look into his empty gray eyes. I close one eyelid and then the other and shush whatever may be left of him into eternal rest. "I got this now, baby. I got this."

"Somebody get my mom out of here," Michael says. Looking up, I find everybody's position has changed. The women are largely removed from the space now, standing back behind their men. This isn't a rescue anymore, but a massacre. I carefully extract myself from beneath Jim's body and place his

Cease (the Bayonet Scars finale)

head gently on the cement. Jeremy approaches me, but my face and gun encourage him not to.

"I'm here, baby," I say to my youngest son as I push my way through the men. Ryan's the last in my way, but I don't push him. I only have to gently sneak by, and he lets me go. My heart is breaking into tiny little pieces that can't be collected and put back together. And it's fine and I don't care, because the only thing I had to stay together for anymore just took his final breath. Still, I push on.

Michael stands, with Leo by his side, in front of his father's men. In front of Michael is his father. He's got his knees to the ground with his legs tucked beneath him. His head is bowed. Execution style, only he's made to face his own men. If it weren't for the tremble of Mike's hand, I might think he was sedated somehow. Not that anybody here would give him that courtesy. He needs to feel every single piece of the pain he's about to endure.

"There's a new boss at the helm," Michael says. His shiny gold Desert Eagle looks heavy in his hand as the barrel points at the back of his father's head. Maybe it's not the gun itself but the act instead. I don't care either way. Mike took my babies. Jim helped me save them twenty years later. And now here we are. So many are dead, and those who are left are hurting. My attention shifts for half a moment to the curvy woman in the corner of the warehouse. She's got her hand over her mouth and her eyes clamped closed.

Gloria.

I want to comfort her, if only to focus on something other than my own pain, but my body won't let me. Instead, I stand, glued in place, as I watch my baby boy deliver a speech to a crowd of frightened men. They don't show it much, but it's there in the ticks of their jaws and the flickering of their eyes. Dead men always know what's coming.

"I will not stand for loyalty to anyone but me, is that understood?"

One lone man steps forward, despite the multitude of guns pointed in his direction. He spits on the cement and snarls in Michael's direction as he says, "I answer only to your father."

In response, Michael winks at the man and then pulls the trigger. His .38 lands center in the back of Mike's skull. His body slumps forward, death immediately taking him. I feel nothing. Where I should feel relief and vengeance, I just feel even more sorrow. Michael's face is impassive, as though he didn't just put a bullet in the back of his father's skull. The man who challenged him takes off running, but he doesn't get far. Without pause, Michael takes him out with three bullets to the guy's back.

"Does anybody else want to challenge me?"

Nobody does. They all stand in silence at my son's feet. Leo takes to one knee in a show of fealty that I've never before seen in the Italians. It doesn't take long for the wary and fearful men to do the same. As I scan the room, watching each of Mike's, now Michael's, men pledge their loyalty to him, a sinking horror overtakes me.

This might be the end of the war for Forsaken, but it's just the beginning for Michael. He won't ever give up his position of power, and he won't leave New York even if I ask, so I won't. Instead, I stand by his side, terrified to look him in the eye and discover that he's more his father than I ever realized—a merciless killer with no remorse for any of his sins.

The End
Exactly three years after our journey began, we now end it with Cease. Thank you for joining me on this epic ride.

CHAPTER TWENTY-THREE

Now Presenting Mr. & Mrs. Stone

Ryan
Fort Bragg, California
A few years later

The icy wind cuts through my thin black button-up and practically leaves icicles on my arms in its wake. It's not so bad on my chest and back, where my cut provides a little extra protection, but the rest of me is covered in goosebumps. Even my rather sizable nut sack has shrunk to something less than impressive. Still, I don't move. I'd have been warmer if I'd worn flannel, but I promised my dad I wouldn't.

Give her what she wants. You won't ever regret making her happy.

Cub asked for the button-up. The cut, the jeans, the boots were all fine. But the plain black button-up was a must. After years of being turned inside out by this woman, of begging her to wear my ring, she finally accepted. If all she wants is one fucking thing, I'll do it. Hell, I'd have worn a full monkey suit if she'd ask me to. But she didn't, because that's my girl. She doesn't ask for more than she needs.

And in just a few minutes, my girl becomes my wife.

My nerves get the best of me, and I have to suck in a shaky breath to calm myself down. It doesn't work, but at least when I scrub my face I can get rid of the water in my eyes without feeling like such a pussy. I wish my dad were here. I wish so fucking bad that I'd have taken that bullet instead.

I love my girl. She's pesky and pushy and wormed her way into my heart. I didn't even know I *could* feel this way, and I'm still not entirely sure it's healthy. It's got to be a sickness, right? This constant need to touch her, to hear her voice, and to see her must be the result of some kind of fever that melted my brain. Best fucking thing that ever happened to me. Meeting my mom and brother are a close second, but my girl fucking takes it.

"If you're having second thoughts, don't bother jumping. I'll just push you off myself." Ma carefully navigates the rocks and climbs her way up to where I'm sitting. I turn toward her, my heart in my throat as she makes her way to me in those fucking heeled boots she has on. We're close to the cliff, and it's a steep drop. I'm not ready to bury another parent. If she goes overboard, I'm just gonna go ahead and throw myself over after her.

"Last thing on my mind," I say once she's settled beside me.

"So then what are you doing all the way out here when you're getting married in five minutes?"

"Thinking." She doesn't push my answer. That's the thing about my mom. She never pushes me to be somebody I'm not. Ever since the first day I met her, she's always just accepted who I am. If I'm a dick, she's cool with it. If I'm an unforgivable monster, she finds a way to justify it. She does the same with Ian, and she did the same with Dad. "I miss him."

Ma nods. She sniffles, but I don't look at her. My throat is closed up, and my hands are shaking again, but this time not from the cold. If I see my mother crying, I'm going to lose my shit.

"So do I, baby. Jim would've liked to see this. You in a button-up. Alex in a dress. He was so happy at Ian and Mindy's wedding. I know he's sad that he's not here."

"You talk about him like he's not dead," I say in a much harsher tone than I intend.

"Because for me, he's not dead. I know where his body is buried. I picked out the headstone, remember? But Jim's body was only part of him. Your dad's spirit? That hasn't gone anywhere."

"You're crazy, Ma. He's still dead."

Reaching over, she pats my knee and rests her head on my arm. She does this shit all the time—always hugging me and finding small ways to touch me as a means of giving me comfort without being too overt. I take it for granted, she does it so much. But right now it means the world to me. Dad patted my shoulder a lot. He'd squeeze the back of my neck in greeting, just so I'd know he was there. My head drops, and I squeeze my eyes shut. My throat constricts around what feels like a fucking golf ball. And of course, because it's my mother next to me, she has to cuddle closer and hum the same fucking tune she used to make us feel better when we were kids. Dad used to mimic her for fun, and he was terrible at it. He never could make it sound even half as good, but fuck, he tried. On the nights when Ian couldn't sleep and the terrors got to be too much, he'd scream. Those were the nights when I'd go and lie next to him in his bed until he calmed down. If he couldn't stop screaming, eventually Dad would make his way in there. And if all else failed, Mom would come in clutch.

Tears well in my eyes. Not a single one falls before Ma notices and decides to make it worse by telling me her favorite memory of us together. I was nine and called her "Mom" for the first time. It was intentional, she remembers that much, but doesn't remember everything else. Unlike her, I vividly remember every detail of that day. That was the day I finally got a mom.

Fuck.

I don't even try to hide the tears now. I've cried four times in my life that I can remember. Once was when my grandma died, the second when Mancuso cut up Cub's face, the third when my dad died, and then now. I didn't even cry a few weeks ago when we found out we're going to have a baby. I was just happy then. It's about fucking time I knocked her up—I've been playing fast and loose with the condoms for almost a year now.

"I think you're trying to kill me," I say when Ma finishes.

She laughs softly. "A mother's greatest joy is finding new ways to emotionally devastate her children."

"Then you must be the happiest fuck alive."

"Sometimes I am," she says. "Like now. You're officially late to your own wedding, punk."

We wipe away our tears once we're safely away from the edge of the cliff. I'm still freezing. I think my man nipples could cut glass right now, but my heart hurts too much to pay it any mind. I give the cliff one last look and head toward the fence that separates Forsaken's property from city land. The ocean side of the fence is covered in hundreds of white Christmas tree lights that are collectively bright enough so that we can be married by the ocean without any ugly barriers in the way. We didn't exactly get a permit for it—and by that I mean Alex asked me to, and I said I did even though I didn't because fuck the city and fuck that shit. Forsaken doesn't ask permission.

"You're late, fucker," Ian says as I rush past him and the rows of folding chairs that are filled with our family and friends. I give him the bird on my way to the altar but stop short. Off to the side, in a big, poofy white dress is my girl. She's huddled with her twin, Michael, and laughing about something. When he notices me watching, he gives her a nudge. My girl stands there in her wedding dress like it's no big deal. But it's a very big deal. She's gorgeous. I close the distance between us and cup her face in my hand. The rough skin of her scars reminds me of all she's endured and all that we've lost. With my other hand, I rub her still-flat belly to remind myself of all that we still have.

"Have you been crying?" she asks in a hushed tone.

"I miss my dad," I admit. I've been working on being more honest with her. It's not easy, and most days I don't even try, but it's our wedding day. I won't be pissing her off before this thing is legal.

"I miss him, too," she says with a sad smile. And then she kisses me. We're not married yet, but I'm

Cease (the Bayonet Scars finale)

happy to wait a few more minutes if it means I get to spend that time kissing my girl.

CHAPTER TWENTY-FOUR

And it Never Ends...

Ruby
And several years after that...

"Ma!" Ryan shouts through the open kitchen window. I huff and meet his eyes. He's no more than twenty feet from me, but he insists on yelling. Some things never change. My boy stands at the large stainless steel grill, flipping burgers and hot dogs. He's got the same loaded expression on his face that he did the day I met him. That was something like thirty years ago now. It's only in moments like these that I remember I didn't give birth to him. Growing frustrated, he shouts again. "Ma! Come on, I need the fucking patties."

Smiling smugly, I raise my glass of whiskey to him and mutter, "You can wait, you impatient little punk," and take a swig of the brown liquor.

Life is calmer now. Ryan's not. It's easy, or easier at least. But Ryan *is* less difficult. Having twins that act just like him has pretty much limited the energy he has to expel bitching at people for the most random of shit. That and the fact that now that bud's legal in California, he can pretty much just stay high. At least it mellows his ass out some. The club's had to find other ways to supplement the loss we've taken on our profits due to taxes. Still, we've fared better than other businesses, so we make due. The Fort Bragg charter is bigger now. With less violence and risk, our members have hung around longer than they used to. Slowly, we're becoming a retirement destination for aging Forsaken.

I think I knew I was officially old the day Wyatt and Amber's son, Zander, patched in. It doesn't matter that Zander is as big as his dad now—I'll still always see him as the smart-mouthed teenager he was when he first came into my life. Nowadays, he's more likely to be found eyeing Izzy Phillips than he is acting like a punk kid. Like he is now, I think with a smile out the window at Zander. The boy is almost thirty, so he's more man than anything. At twenty-four, Izzy is old enough to know what she's getting into with Zander. And judging by the looks she's giving him when she thinks he isn't looking, they're going to be getting into something soon. A few feet behind Izzy stands Elle, her older sister, and Amber, Zander's mom. Both women are staring the couple down, practically shooting daggers at the kids. I let out a soft sigh and snort.

"I know this is you," I say to an empty room. My eyes fall closed for a moment, and I let the silence surrounding me sink in. Jim's been gone for over ten years now, but I hear his voice just as clearly as I did the day he died. He laughs—at least in my head he does. And it's fucking beautiful. My life is busier than my kids think it should be, so I don't get to hear Jim's voice as much as I used to, so I relish these times of quiet. "You're getting those women back for being a pain in your ass when they were younger."

"Hey, Pop! You want to quit distracting Mom from making the hamburger patties so your son can chill out, please?" I turn in place to find Alex standing on the other side of the breakfast bar. Her brown eyes dance as she shakes her head at me. It's no secret that I talk to Jim. It's kind of a joke at this point. I just don't tell them that I know he can hear me. I don't know about God or church or any of that shit, but I know my man hasn't left me alone.

"He can wait," I say and take another sip, emptying my glass. The front door opens and then slams closed. Little feet stomp inside in a dramatic huff. My sweet Esme practically throws herself into the room. With the way she acts, you'd think she's eighteen and not eight. Her near-black hair is piled high atop her head, and her wide gray eyes are shooting daggers at her mother.

"What's up, Chicken Butt?" Alex says, turning her attention to her daughter. Alex isn't even remotely fazed by her daughter's attitude. She gets it enough at home from both the girl and her father that she can't afford to get riled up every single time somebody pitches a fit.

"*Your* husband won't stop complaining about how long Grandma's taking," Esme says to her mother before turning away. Sitting herself down in the chair across from me, she stares at me blankly.

"Hey, you blame your grandpa for that one," I say, picking up the speed of my patty-making.

"Thanks, Grandpa," Esme shouts with her eyes fixed on the ceiling.

"Would you crazies stop talking to Grandpa and get the damn patties made already?" My grandson sticks his head in the window and gives us a warning look, like his eight-year-old ass can do something about it if we don't. He's the spitting image of his twin sister. All dark hair and gray eyes with a complexion that seems to shift between olive and a pale pink.

Alex's and Esme's heads whip around so quickly that if I didn't know better, I'd think they might be possessed. Alex's scar catches the light, and it looks just as angry and painful as it did the day she was released from the hospital all those years ago. My daughter takes too long with her response. It's Esme who responds with, "Shut up, Michael." Even knowing they named him after his uncle, hearing my grandson's given name sometimes throws me off. We normally call him Track because he can outrun just about anybody he comes across. While Esme, in honor of her mother, gets called Queenie.

Looking out the window again, I watch Track rush off to bitch to his father about our speed or lack thereof. My smile brightens when I see Ian and Mindy approach with the kids. After Chel died a few years ago, they took in Xavier and DJ, who are now thirteen and six. It was tragic the way we lost her. Marks lost control of his bike when they were on a ride up the coast. Chel and the baby didn't make it. Marks did, until he couldn't take any more and took his own life six months later. He was a good man who loved Chel with his whole heart. Did right by her. Married her, treated Xavier as his own, had DJ, and was expecting a little girl. But sometimes that's just how life is. It takes the best ones early and leaves the rest of us to suffer the consequences.

Out in the distance, closer to the barn, are Wyatt, Grady, Jeremy, and Diesel. They have a few prospects with them, including Chief's son, Stephen. Duke and Nic sit side by side at a picnic table with their daughter Robin, who's a teenager now. On the opposite side is Cheyenne, who's about to give birth to her and Jeremy's son any day. Their toddler-aged daughter, Haley, sits between Chey and her grandma, Holly. My line of sight follows Track, running around in the distance, being chased by Charlie and Jim, Grady and Holly's kids. Once, a few years ago, I made a joke about the growing size of the Forsaken family, to which Amber announced she was pregnant again. It was right before Elle and Diesel started trying, but after one miscarriage, they decided not to go through that again.

Ryan stomps in the house with his mini-me son hot on his heels and shakes his head at the stack of patties in front of me. I've been done for almost five minutes now, but I wasn't about to rush them out to Mr. Temper Tantrum. Even if he is damn cute when he's acting a fool.

"Al, I think you need another baby," I say. My eyes are on Ryan, but my comment is for his wife. I'm smiling like a goofball, fondly remembering the day the twins were born.

Alex snorts in response and starts telling me how that's not going to happen in a variety of ways. Ryan moves behind Alex and holds her against him. Softly, he places a kiss to the scar between her eye and ear. He does this a lot, touching her scars, kissing them. He never shies away from them or seems to think she's any less beautiful with them. If anything, she's more beautiful, I think. I can't help but watch this man and woman who remind me so much of me and Jim. I love my kids, I love my family, and I love this club. There will always be violence and danger on the periphery. That's life when you live outside the bounds of the law. But there's also loyalty and pride. And family.

A black suit comes into view, blocking my sight line of the kids off in the distance. I blink, my eyes trailing up the long torso, and nearly burst into tears at the sight before me. His olive skin is darker than the last time I saw him, but that's to be expected in summer. His brown eyes dance, almost exactly like his sister's did just a few minutes ago.

"Come on, Mom," Michael says. "You didn't think I'd miss my niece and nephew's birthday, did you?"

My eyes fall closed for half a moment as I tell Jim I miss him—silently this time—and suck in a breath. Alex is screaming in excitement, and my boys are rushing to the house to meet their brother.

"I miss you, baby," I whisper to myself as I watch the kids flock to our newest arrival. A cool wind picks up out of nowhere and engulfs me. I revel in it, knowing that it's my man's way of saying, *"Miss you, too, momma."*

Wars begin, nobody knowing the devastation they'll cause. Blood will be shed, people will be lost, and when it all settles, nobody will ever be the same. There will always be violence and hate—and death. But there will also always be love.

And family.

And it never ends.

ABOUT THE AUTHOR

As a child, JC was fascinated by things that went bump in the night. As they say, some things never change. JC is known for her bad-ass anti-heroes who lure unsuspecting readers into their dark stories and refuse to leave them alone-- even once their story is finished. JC is a San Francisco Bay Area native, but has also called both Texas and Louisiana home. She just recently ditched her flip flops for winter boots and now resides in Southwestern Illinois. When she's not torturing her characters for fun, JC drops the pen name and goes by Christina. JC is the author of the Bayonet Scars series-- about an outlaw motorcycle club that starts a war with the Italian mafia. Now that she's retiring her bikers, she's seriously pondering what's next for the Mancuso crime family.

Made in the USA
Columbia, SC
14 June 2019